DIG ME A GRAVE

by

JOHN SPAIN

www.wildsidepress.com

COPYRIGHT, 1942 BY E. P. DUTTON & CO., INC.
COPYRIGHT, 1943 BY CRESTWOOD PUBLISHING CO., INC.,
NEW YORK, N. Y.

*All rights reserved, including the right to
reproduce this book, or portions
thereof, in any form.*

BLACK CAT DETECTIVE SERIES

IT is the aim of the Publishers to bring to the public from time to time, inexpensive editions of better detective mystery novels to be known as the BLACK CAT DETECTIVE SERIES.

THIS mystery thriller was originally published by *E. P. Dutton & Co., Inc.,* at $2.00.

CHAPTER 1

RYE held the letter gingerly, as though momentarily expecting it to bite him. It was not his letter. It belonged to Callahan, behind the big desk in the middle of the heavily ornate office. The letter had been written by a woman who presumably was now dead. Rye felt a little as though he were holding a bit of ectoplasm in his hand, only this was unlike the usual ectoplasm produced by mediums. It had all the inherent qualities of dynamite.

"You see the spot I'm in," Callahan said. He was a large man with a square florid face and thinning iron gray hair. Strong square-tipped fingers bent a bronze letter opener into the shape of a horse shoe. He sighed. "I wish I could go down there myself."

"Like hell you do," Rye said. He regarded his employer without love. "Just what am I expected to do with this girl if I find her?"

Callahan looked uncomfortable. "Well — " He stood up violently. "God damn it, if she really is my daughter I owe her something, don't I?"

"I wouldn't know," Rye said. "I never had a daughter." After a while he said thoughtfully, "Not even an illegitimate daughter." He was a tall young man with very dark hair and eyes and the slightly disreputable look of a satyr. His clothes looked as though he had slept in them. He had. This was partially the result of having gotten terrifically drunk the night before, but he excused that on the grounds that he wouldn't have gotten drunk at all if he hadn't had to look for Gerald. Gerald was another offspring of Edward Callahan, only Gerald was legitimate. Rye felt that it was a little unfair of Callahan to be running in a new family for him, William Rye, to get out of jams. "I think I'll join the navy," he said.

Callahan glared at him. "You fool, you already have joined the navy! But you're not sober enough yet to know it."

Rye looked surprised. "Have I?" He remembered that he was indeed an officer in the Naval Reserve. He was supposed to be a Naval Intelligence officer, because in his extreme youth he had once served a hitch aboard a destroyer and had later become a detective. The combination had appealed to Washington in the National Emergency, but not enough to give him an assignment after making him an officer. While waiting for Washington to remember him he was still attached to Callahan, and Callahan's family, and Callahan's private and public interests. People spoke of him as Callahan's trouble-shooter. He preferred the more dignified title of Confidential Agent. He re-read the letter: ". . . For myself I do not ask you anything — ever. But for our daughter, yes. I am dying. My husband, he is not a good man. So I fear for Carmelita, and what happens to her when I am gone." The letter was postmarked Santa Caterina, State of Sinaloa, Mexico. It had been forwarded many times, because there were a lot of Edward Callahans in Los Angeles, California.

Rye made disparaging noises. "What would Sybil say if she knew?" Sybil was Callahan's wife.

"You know Sybil as well as I do," Callahan said bitterly. He was impelled to add, "Or almost as well." He crossed to the tall windows and looked down on ten o'clock morning traffic. "It isn't only that, though. The opposition papers, and Granger, would like nothing better than to crucify me, and, by inference, the Governor."

Rye had already considered these things. Callahan was by way of being the political boss of the state, and there were certain elements who professed to believe that he even used the state to further the interests of Calexico Oil and affiliated companies. Notably there was Weldon Granger who, under the guise of a public benefactor, aspired to become boss himself. "Why don't you just send her some money?"

Callahan turned. "You're not being very bright this morning. How do I know she's my kid? How do I know it isn't a trap of some kind? And even is she is my kid, how can I be sure the money wouldn't fall into the wrong hands?" He waved at the letter. "This — this stepfather or whatever he is? Suppose he's not only a bastard, but a smart bastard. What a hold over me a pay-off would give him!" After a while, not looking at Rye, he said, "You think I'm a heel, don't you?"

"No."

Callahan shrugged his heavy shoulders. "Then you're the only one that doesn't." He went back and sat at the desk. "You've been with me a long time, Bill. You're probably the only guy I've ever opened up to, and that's because I've never had the feeling you had a knife up your sleeve." He drew in a slow breath. "Even Sybil and Gerald only stick to me for what they can get out of me."

Rye's mouth drooped. "The great are always lonely — it says here." He found a crumpled cigarette in one of his crumpled pockets, massaged it back into something like a semblance of its original shape, looked at it and finally decided that he didn't want it after all. He hurled it into a wastebasket. "You'd better tell me a little more about this business, Ed."

Callahan brightened. "Then you'll go?"

"Good old Rye," Rye said. "Always the sucker."

Callahan took up the letter. His mouth lost something of its hardness and his eyes softened in retrospect. "That must have been all of eighteen, nineteen years ago — I was supposed to be a heller with the women then."

"And married," Rye said.

"Well, yes," Callahan admitted. He made an impatient gesture. "Though that part of it needn't enter into it. You know Sybil."

Rye did indeed know Sybil. She was really a charming woman. At the moment she was charming a man named Harris Friedlander, who was one of Callahan's attorneys. She had even tried to charm William Rye. Motherhood sat very lightly on Sybil Callahan.

"I think perhaps Carmel Machado was the only woman I ever really loved," Callahan said.

Rye bent and retrieved the cigarette from the wastebasket. "So you ran away and left her."

"There was Sybil," Callahan pointed out. "And Gerald." After a while he said, "Besides, I was after bigger things than love, then." He frowned. "Now I've got them I don't know what to do with them" — his mouth was suddenly a firm hard line — "except keep 'em." He leaned back in his chair, looking at Rye from beneath half-lowered lids. "I wish I could see my — this girl."

"All right," Rye said, "go down there."

"I can't." Callahan shook himself, like a Saint Bernard coming out of the water. "Besides the possibility that it's a political trap, Mexico is a ticklish situation right now. I'd be accused of trying to foment a revolution or something, to get back some of the properties Expropriation took away from us."

"Same thing applies to me, doesn't it? I'm known to be working for you."

Callahan stood up. "You know how to handle these things better than I do." Something that could have been sincere admiration came into his eyes. "You've been able to keep Sybil and Gerald out of the papers for the last two or three years."

"And Calexico Oil," Rye said modestly, adding, "Except in a nice way, of course."

"You'll need some money," Callahan said presently. He stopped his pacing and went back to the desk and drew a check on one of his private accounts. "Get me a picture of the girl. I can tell from that. Afterward we can figure out some way to fix her up without letting her know where it came from." He put his gray eyes on Rye in a direct stare. "Without letting anyone know."

Rye exhaled a cloud of blue smoke. "You're almost certain right now, aren't you?"

"No."

"I wish I could be as sure of going to Heaven," Rye said. He crushed the cigarette out in a tray. "If you ask me, this is going to turn out to be dynamite."

"I didn't ask you," Callahan said stubbornly. And then, ashamed of himself, "No, I'm sorry I said that, Bill." He was almost diffident when he said, "I don't know how I can explain it to you, boy. I've probably wrecked a hundred men in my time. A few women too. But this is — well, this is just different, that's all."

The telephone buzzed gently. Callahan picked it up. "Yes? Oh, hello, Powers." Frowning, he motioned Rye not to go away. "The hell you say! What kind of a check?" His scowl grew darker as he listened to the voice at the other end of the wire. "I don't care, damn it. I told you I didn't want him playing over your tables any more. No, I won't make it good." He put the phone against his chest and glared at Rye. "Gerald again!"

Rye's face was impassive as he picked up the extension. "Hello, Pat."

"Oh, it's you!" Powers said. His voice held a nice sharp edge. Powers was not the oily-smooth type of gambler. He was a businessman. "One of my dealers took the kid's check for five grand. It bounced. I want my dough."

"All right," Rye said.

Callahan yelped. "If he gets it you'll pay it out of your own pocket, by God!"

"I don't care who pays it," Powers retorted. "Just so it's paid."

"Sure, Pat," Rye said. "Yes, I'll see that it's taken care of. This morning." He looked at Callahan's congested face. "Well, you know how it is. Or you would if you were Gerald's father."

"God forbid!" Power said fervently.

Callahan banged the phone down, almost deafening Rye and probably Pat Powers, too. Rye waited for the echoes of the racket to subside. "Just the same, Pat, maybe it would be a good idea to warn your dealers off. The bartenders too," he added gently.

"Don't think I won't, pal."

"Good," Rye said. After a moment he said, "How's Blossom?"

"She's got a hangover," Powers grumbled.

Rye was politely sympathetic. "So have I. You might tell her I inquired, anyway." He disconnected. There was mild reproof in his eyes when he again looked at Callahan, who was wrestling violently with a frayed cigar. "You should never tell a gambler you won't pay off. Especially a gambler like Powers. He can be very bad medicine."

Callahan was outraged. "God damn it, I told him — "

"I know you did," Rye said patiently. He went over to the water cooler and drank three glasses of water, one right after the other. He experienced a mild sensation of drowning. "Naturally other people aren't as interested in chastening your son as we are."

"Well — "

"Besides," Rye said, "Powers swings quite a pocketful of votes. We wouldn't want him making a deal with Granger." He coughed. "Or would we?"

Callahan scowled at him. "Sometimes I wonder whether it's me running this state or you." Nevertheless he seized a pen and wrote another check. This one was for five thousand dollars, though it was notable that he did not make it out to Pat Powers. He made it out to William Rye.

"Face," Rye said, folding the check. "Save it while you may."

Callahan flushed. "You say the damnedest things!" He remembered something from the Powers conversation. "Who's Blossom?"

"Pat's mistress," Rye said. "Ostensibly she is a singer." He pretended to find something of great interest in the tips of his shoes. "Blossom Dee is another reason I thought we ought to be nice to Powers. Gerald likes her."

"My God!"

"Yes," Rye said. "Sometimes I feel like that too." His face assumed a mask of pleased surprise as the door opened and Sybil Callahan came in. Behind his back his fingers whisked Carmel Machado's letter from the desk. "Well, Sybil!"

She was in caracul this morning. Perfectly coiffed platinum hair supported an inconsequential fluff of the same material, meant to be a hat. She was tall for a woman, and strikingly beautiful if you happened to like perfection. She had lovely ankles. "Hello, William." She turned wide-set blue eyes on her husband. "First of the month, darling. I just dropped in for my check."

"I left it on your dressing table," Callahan said.

"You did? I didn't see it." She lifted the phone and called the number of the big house in Bel Air. "Ellen? Will you look in my dressing room for a check Mr. Callahan is supposed to have left for me?" She waited, drumming impatient beautifully gloved fingers on the desk, quite aware of the regal picture she made. Like motherhood, her forty years sat very lightly on Sybil Callahan. She could have been no more than thirty. Presently she said, "No, it isn't important, Ellen. Thank you." She replaced the phone and looked at Callahan. "It isn't there. Do you suppose that Gerald — ?"

Callahan's growl was that of an enraged bulldog. "I'll break his God damned neck!" He seized the phone and called his bank and gave orders to stop the check. "And I'll want to know what endorsements appear on it!"

Rye said, "Well, if you'll excuse me," and moved toward the door. "Nice seeing you again, Sybil."

Callahan's voice stopped him. "About that other matter — "

"I'll see what I can do," Rye promised him gravely. He went out into the anteroom, closing the heavy door behind him so that the Callahan family's private affairs wouldn't become any more public than they were already.

From her desk by the windows Miss Sheridan McKay regarded him searchingly. "You look terrible," she finally decided.

"I feel terrible," Rye confessed. He pointed a finger at her. "You'd look terrible too if you had to go through what I do." His mind was busy with the problem of Gerald Callahan. The problem of Carmelita Machado, or Carmelita Ruiz, together with other possible illegitimate children of Callahan's, would have to go till later. He bent and kissed the back of Miss McKay's neck. "How do you feel about marrying me this morning?"

Miss McKay pretended to be puzzled. "Do you mean marrying you this morning, or just feeling about it this morning?" She was really quite attractive, even when pretending to be puzzled. Her hair was almost as dark as Rye's, though in the bright sun it had highlights of rich mahogany. Sometimes her eyes were gray, sometimes almost the color of topaz. Always they made William Rye vaguely uncomfortable. Under certain conditions they even made him wish that he had led a better life. "You'll be sorry," he said. "People are always sorry when they don't marry me."

She looked at him. "What's wrong with Sybil this time?"

"Does something always have to be wrong with her?"

"Something usually is," Miss McKay said dryly.

Rye looked around for his hat. "Maybe it's that time of life," he said. He went out and through the busy general offices of Calexico Oil, and caught a down elevator to the ground floor. In a phone booth in the lobby drug store he began calling numbers where he thought young Gerald Callahan might be located.

CHAPTER 2

RYE came into Luigi's with every sign of a man in dire need of a drink. It had taken him two hours to find Gerald Callahan, but now that he had found him he expressed great astonishment, conveying the impression that it was entirely a matter of chance. "Well, Gerald!"

The boy was sitting on one of the tall bar stools, not drinking anything, just sitting there. Around and about him there was quite a crowd of the usual mob who had to fortify their stomachs to withstand lunch, but Gerald was on a little island all his own. He appeared wrapped in gloom. His mouth was sullen. "What do you want?"

Rye brightened. "Is that an invitation to a drink?"

"It's an invitation to get out and leave me alone."

"All right," Rye said amiably. He turned away, paused as though at an afterthought. "By the way, I squared that bum check you gave Pat Powers."

Gerald scowled. "What are you trying to do, make me feel like a heel?" Curiosity stirred the dull muddiness of his eyes. "I suppose he called up the old man?"

"Well, yes," Rye admitted.

The boy's mouth became even more sullen. He was only twenty-one. Very light hair, almost as light as his mother's, was rumpled under a hat that looked as though an elephant had stepped on it. Except for the muddiness occasioned by last night's debauch he had his father's eyes. "He cut off my allowance."

"The old man?" Rye laughed easily. "Don't let that worry you. Any time you need a few dollars I'm a sucker for a touch." He ordered a straight Scotch from a passing bartender. "The only thing is," he said carelessly, "I'm going to be out of town for a few days, so if you think you're liable to get in any jams you might let me know now."

Gerald looked at him. "Take me with you."

Something besides the straight Scotch made Rye cough. "You wouldn't be interested this time." He had the odd feeling that this was his own son he was talking to, though that was obviously ridiculous; scarcely ten years separated them. He wished Callahan had the capacity to make friends with the boy. "You see your mother this morning?"

"No."

"You didn't even look in on her?"

Gerald's mouth drooped. "You don't know Sybil if you think anybody can look in on her in the morning. She throws things."

Rye nodded. "That's probably what she did with the check." He finished his drink, making a wry face over it. "And then forgot all about it."

The boy's lips drew back over even white teeth. His voice was harsh. "What check was that?"

"One the old man is supposed to have left on her dressing table."

The muddiness that was in the boy's eyes spread all over his face. "You think I took it," he said thickly.

"No."

"But *he* thinks so."

"Your father is not always as bright as he should be," Rye admitted. "There was some talk about breaking your naughty word neck."

Gerald bridled. "Let him try it!"

Rye shook his head. "You guys both ought to quit acting like children." He massaged his chin with lean brown fingers. "Callahan really isn't a bad fellow when you get to know him."

"And how do you do that?" Gerald asked bitterly.

"I did it," Rye said. He grinned. "Took me a few years, but it just goes to show what can be done." He put a hand in his pocket. "How about a little loan to tide you over?"

Hot blood flooded the young man's face. "Well, if you could spare a couple hundred — "

"Sure," Rye said. He produced some crumpled bills and laid them on the bar. Then, very casually, he said, "Powers was kind of burned up about the check, pal. I just thought you ought to know that he's a tough hombre to have sore at you."

"I'm through with him," Gerald said.

"Good." Rye made little rings on the mahogany with his empty glass. "Blossom Dee is his property too, Gerry."

"That's what he thinks."

Rye sighed. "Well, I just thought I'd call it to your attention." He held out his hand. "Try to get along with the old man for a few days, will you, chum? At least while I'm gone."

The boy's mouth softened. "For a wet nurse you're not a bad guy, Bill."

"And stay out of jail," Rye said. He turned and went down the long narrow crowded room toward the street doors. Harris Friedlander was just coming in. Friedlander was a lean handsome Jew with hard bright eyes and the quick, nervous manner of one who is constantly and consciously one jump ahead of you, no matter what you're thinking. He was a brilliant attorney. The carnation in his buttonhole gave his otherwise careful dress an air of foppishness. "Hello, Fried," Rye said. "Didn't I see you dancing with Sybil the other night?"

The hard bright eyes examined him. "Anything is possible." Thin lips curved upward in a sudden smile that just missed being a sneer. "I had Callahan's permission. Do I have to get yours too?"

"You could have picked a better place, is all," Rye said. "Like Caesar's, the wife of the governor's friend shouldn't be caught dead in a dump like the Black Cat." He looked at the palm of his hand. "Not that I'm trying to tell you what to do, you understand."

Friedlander's mobile mouth curved the other way, downward, as though he had just bitten into something unpleasant. "I'll try to be more circumspect in the future, Mr. Rye." Hate burned in his bright dark eyes. He went on to the bar without another word.

Rye stood there a moment, thinking. Finally he entered a phone booth and called the Callahan house. Sybil came on the wire presently. "Bill, how thoughtful of you!"

Rye's eyes narrowed slightly. He made his voice deliberate. "About that check," he said. "You probably know by this time that you'd better find it, but I just thought I'd tell you."

She was on the verge of hysteria. "Gerald took it!"

"No."

"But Bill, what'll I do?"

He frowned at the transmitter. "Somebody blackmailing you?"

There was the briefest of hesitations. Then she said, "Certainly not!" with a very fair imitation of outraged virtue. "Whatever gave you that idea?"

"You don't have to pretend with me, Sybil," Rye said tiredly. After a moment he added, "Nor with Ed, either, for that matter. We both know you for what you are. The only thing is, we ought to keep the rest of the world from knowing it." He drew an uneven breath. "That would hurt Ed, and I won't stand for that."

"You're cruel!"

He ignored that. "What's the guy's name?" She gave it to him. "All right," he said, "I'll take care of it." He whistled part of a little tune between his teeth. "Meantime you'd better call Ed and tell him you found the check." He hung up and went out to the street and flagged down a cab.

The address given him by Sybil turned out to be one of the new flash apartments off of Vermont south of Wilshire. Rye went into the small, cloister-like lobby, ran his eye along the row of brass mailboxes till he found the right one. Then, ignoring that, he pressed half a dozen buzzers indiscriminately until the inner door-latch clicked. He let himself in and went up heavily carpeted stairs to the second floor. He was breathing evenly, carefully, and his eyes were watchful when presently he knocked on the door of 232.

The man who opened the door smelled of lilac vegetal. A gust of it preceded him through the opening, twitching Rye's nostrils. "Well?" He was a small, round-bodied man of indeterminate age. He had practically no hair and his eyes were the pinkish eyes of a ferret. He kept one hand in the pocket of his purple silk robe. "Well?" he said again. You could see he wasn't going to like William Rye.

"Are you Mr. Ambrose?"

"Unh-hunh."

"Mr. Walter Ambrose?" Rye insisted.

The small man's mouth tightened. So did his hand on whatever it was he had in the pocket of the robe. "Are you trying to kid somebody, chum?"

Rye took out Callahan's check, the one made out to himself. He held it just far enough away from the small man's eyes so that it couldn't be read. "Does that look like I'm kidding?" He put the edge of the check against his lips and whistled a few bars of Melancholy Baby. "I was instructed to buy something with this."

Ambrose released his hold on the doorknob. "Come in." He stood aside, giving Rye access to the small foyer and, beyond that, a modernistic living room that had been allowed to get pretty sloppy looking. On a cluttered table there were a couple of expensive German midget cameras and some rolls of film. Through a partially open door came the smell of a photographic darkroom. In spite of the check, possibly because of it, Ambrose was still cagey. "What are you supposed to be buying?"

"Pictures, I think," Rye said.

"Whose?"

"A lady named Sybil Callahan asked me to see you."

Ambrose half lowered his eyes. "You a mouthpiece?"

"Maybe."

"Then you ought to know I can't take checks."

Rye nodded. "I didn't know the exact amount you were asking. When I see what you have we can send a messenger down to the bank."

Ambrose stood there a moment, rocking gently on his small slippered feet. Ferret eyes massaged Rye's person, looking for the tell-tale bulge of a gun. Finally satisfied that there wasn't one he moved crabwise to the windows and risked a quick glance down at the street. Not until then did he take his hand out of the pocket of the robe. "All right, I guess you're on the level. Have a chair for yourself." He disappeared through the door to a bedroom.

Rye did not have a chair. Listening intently he waited until he had counted ten, very slowly. Then, swift and quite sure of himself, he moved to the closed door, opened it and went in. Ambrose was kneeling above a floor safe, disclosed by a rolled-back rug. As Rye's shadow fell on him he twisted to his feet and his right hand dropped an envelope and clawed for the bulge in his pocket. Rye hit him a full-armed blow in the mouth. Rye's left hand clamped down on the half-drawn gun, pushed it and the man's arm around and up behind him. With his right hand he hit Ambrose again and again in the face, until the plump body went limp. A sudden fury burned in him and it was only with a very great effort that he resisted the impulse to expunge the man from the record permanently. He did the next best thing. He emptied the safe of perhaps half a dozen envelopes and several rolls of exposed films. He did not look at any of them except the one marked with the name of Callahan. There was only one negative. The three prints had all been made from this. As such pictures went they were not so very bad.

Ambrose groaned and stirred a little as Rye stood up. Almost absently Rye kicked him in the chin. Ambrose quit stirring. Rye went through the apartment unhurriedly but carefully, carrying a wastebasket and accumulating quite a pile of rubbish that would be better if it never saw the light of day. The two cameras he smashed against the andirons in the fireplace. When they were no longer recognizable as cameras he carried them in and laid them on top of the mound beside the floor safe. He then emptied the wastebasket on top of the whole business and lit a match and touched it to the curling end of a roll of film. With a rather pleased expression he watched the fire grow till it was almost a certainty that the entire contents of the bedroom would succumb. He hauled the still somnolent Ambrose into the living room and shut the bedroom door. Presently he shut the hall door too, behind him. Down in the lobby he buzzed the janitor's speaking tube. "I think you've got a fire on the second floor," he said.

CHAPTER 3

THE telephone buzzed gently but inexorably till Rye roused sufficiently to reach out a sleep-drugged hand and lift it vaguely in the direction of his mouth. "Yes?"

"Six o'clock, Mr. Rye," the girl on the switchboard downstairs said. She sounded a little annoyed with him for not answering sooner. She didn't feel angelic early in the morning, herself.

"Oh, thanks." He fumbled the instrument back into its cradle without looking at it. A dying sun came in at the windows and pried at his eyelids but he refused to open them. He wondered if he could get from the bedroom through the living room and into the kitchen and make a cup of coffee without opening them. He wished he did not have to go to Mexico to look for a girl named Carmelita. He wished he were not so fond of a man named Edward Callahan.

Over the second cup of coffee, he read about a fire in the apartment of a man named Walter Ambrose. It appeared that the apartment had been practically gutted. Walter Ambrose could give no reason for the fire except that some of his photographic chemicals must have exploded. He was, he said, an amateur photographer. There was no record of his arrest, so it was safe to assume that everything of an incriminating nature had indeed been destroyed. Rye hoped that this would be heartening news to a lot of people besides Sybil Callahan.

The telephone rang again. This time it turned out to be an official of Mexican Airways. He was so sorry, he said, but Mr. Rye's application for a reservation had come in too late. Mr. Rye could not go down to Mazatlan that night, at least by way of Mexican Airways. He was very sorry.

"Well, when can I get a seat?"

"Who knows?" the man said. "Tomorrow, perhaps."

He showered and shaved and dressed, ate a solitary but on the whole satisfactory dinner in the Brown Derby on Wilshire and presently drove the big Buick coupe out to Bel Air. It was eight o'clock when he began the winding ascent of Vallejo Drive. A quarter moon hung poised just above the ridge of the foothills, veiled by a thin fog drifting in from the sea. There was the smell of orange blossoms in the air.

A couple of the estates adjoining Callahan's seemed to have guests for dinner. There were a lot of cars around, big opulent cars, all save one. This was a little car, and shabby according to Bel Air standards, and as Rye's headlights picked it out he saw that there was a man in it, slouched far down in the seat as though desirous of giving the impression that he wasn't there at all. It occurred to Rye that the man might be Mr. Walter Ambrose, bent on reprisal. He swung in between the too ornate gateposts of the Callahan driveway, switched off his lights and retraced his way on foot. When he was exactly opposite the shabby little sedan he paused and appeared to be searching his pockets for a match. Car springs creaked as the man inside shifted his position. Rye crossed the strip of lawn between sidewalk and curb. "Pardon me, have you a match?"

A white blob of face materialized between turned-up coat collar and pulled-down hat. "No." The face did not belong to Mr. Walter Ambrose. Just the same, there was something vaguely familiar about it. Rye leaned a little closer. "A lighter, perhaps?"

"No." And then, as the headlights of a passing car briefly illuminated Rye's own face: "Wait a minute. Ain't I seen you some place before?"

"I've been having a little trouble placing you too," Rye confessed. The unlighted cigarette between his lips waggled tiredly. "The name is Rye."

For a moment there was silence; a kind of palpitant silence, as though the man might be having an internal argument with himself. Fog swooped down, obliterating practically everything but Rye and the shabby little car and the man inside it. Somewhere not too far away there was the sound of voices and car doors banged. The quarter moon gave the fog the substance of skimmed milk. The man in the car made a great business of clearing his throat. "Work for Callahan, don't you?"

"Some," Rye admitted. Something that was not entirely the chill of the fog ran an electric icicle up and down his spine. He was not afraid of the man; rather oddly he had the feeling that the man was afraid of him, and this was always bad. Furtive people, cautious people, especially those lurking in the immediate vicinity of the Callahans, usually spelled trouble of one sort of another for William Rye. He used the hand with the cigarette to push his hat a little farther back on his head. His eyes were sharp and bright and intent, though he kept his voice politely casual. "Something you wanted to see Callahan about?"

Turtle-like, the man's face came out from the shelter of coat collar and hatbrim, bringing it into direct focus. It was not a particularly vicious face. In fact it was not a face you'd remember at all unless there was some very great necessity. The most outstanding thing about it was its almost total lack of color. Even the eyebrows and lashes were pale to the vanishing point. Thin colorless lips finally got around to answering Rye's question. "Damned if I know." And then, enlarging on that, he said in a puzzled voice, "I've got a hunch I've got hold of something, but damned if I know exactly what." He jerked a thumb in the direction of the Callahan driveway. "You know who's up there?" He himself supplied the answer. "The governor!"

A little muscle at the corner of Rye's mouth twitched. "Maybe you'd better tell me about it," he suggested quietly.

"Sure." It was almost as though the man were relieved that the decision had been taken out of his hands. He opened the car door and slid over under the wheel. Rye got in beside him. Briefly the man's hands were busy in his pockets. When presently he switched on the dashlight he had a fistful of cards. Pale, not too well-kept fingers selected one and held it under the light for Rye to read. Like some of the more recent war posters it was practically covered with legends. It said that the Small Detective Agency, Lou Small, Prop., would for a nominal sum conduct secret investigations, locate missing heirs, vanished debtors or even old friends. "It's a slimy racket," Lou Small admitted with admirable candor and without being asked. In extenuation he offered, "A guy's got to live."

Rye said nothing at all. He discovered that Mr. Small's shabby little car made a liar out of Mr. Small. There was a lighter on the instrument panel. He used this to ignite the fog-limp cigarette. He became engrossed in a futile attempt to blow a smoke ring.

Small sighed. "Not a very talkative guy, are you?"

Rye poked a finger through a cloud of smoke, trying to make a ring by artificial means. He was unsuccessful. "I'm a good listener."

Small considered that carefully, from all sides. He expelled a sibilant breath through his thin pale lips. "Well, here it is." Not looking at Rye, not looking at anything in particular, he slid a little farther down under the wheel. "This gal comes into the office this morning and wants me to find a Callahan she thinks used to be in the oil business down in Mexico. Nineteen or twenty years ago."

Again the little muscle at the corner of Rye's mouth began to twitch. He put up a finger and stilled it.

Small's eyes examined him furtively, a little worriedly. "Interested?"

"You haven't said anything yet," Rye said. He flipped the cigarette butt out the window. It lay there in the grass of the parkway, a malicious red eye in the darkness. Presently it winked and was gone. "I can understand why you linked Callahan and the oil business with the Callahan of Calexico Oil."

"Sure. It was a natural."

"You tell the girl about it?"

"No."

"Why not?"

"Well, for one thing," Small said carefully, "I had to do a little checking up to be sure I had the right Callahan." A pale thumb and forefinger picked at the frayed hem of his overcoat, flattened it over his knee. "I've been sitting out here for an hour trying to make up my mind what to do." He half turned in the seat and let Rye see his eyes. "This frail hasn't got much money."

"And Callahan has?"

Small became almost painfully earnest. "Look, I'm in a scabby racket, sure, but I'm not a hog. I just thought it might be worth a little something to your boss not to be found. More'n the ten bucks she gave me."

Rye almost laughed aloud at the irony of it. He had no need to ask who the girl was. The only thing that would have made it funnier, or more tragic, was now no longer necessary. He would not have to go down to Santa Caterina in search of a girl who might or might not be real. He said, "One thing I like about you, Lou, you know your limitations. You're not big time and you've got sense enough to know you never will be big time." His laugh was suddenly brittle. "So you've been sitting out here in the car trying to nerve yourself to go up against someone that is."

Small shivered. "Now look, I don't want no trouble."

"Of course you don't," Rye said cordially. After a while he said, "The lady happen to mention just why she wanted to find a man named Callahan?"

"No." Small's thin lips worried a cigarette out of a crumpled package. "Not that I didn't ask her." With a thumb nail he flicked a match alight and applied it to the fag. "I kind of got the idea she didn't like the guy very well."

No, Rye thought, she wouldn't. If she knows the circumstances she probably hates Callahan's guts. Aloud he said, "I'm not promising you anything, understand. Not until I find out what it's all about." He came to a sudden decision. "Stall her. Tell her you've turned the case over to your partner."

"I ain't got no partner."

"That's where you're wrong," Rye said evenly. "I'm your partner."

CHAPTER 4

VAN SWERINGER let Rye into the hall with his customary and always polite, "How do you do, sir?" Van Sweringen was the Callhan butler and the only thing that ever appeared to ruffle his composure was when some allegedly witty guest would smirk and say, "Not one of *the* Van Sweringens?" Though Sybil would have liked him to, he did not wear livery. He took Rye's coat and hat. "Mr. Callahan is closeted with the governor, sir."

"I'll wait," Rye said. He went down three steps into the enormous sunken living room which looked as though nobody ever really lived in it. Acres and acres of leaf-patterned silvery carpet stretched from wall to wall, and the same silver motif was carried out in the hangings and damask paneling. The room would have been cold as ice were it not for the ruddy warmth of old mahogany. There were some very fine pieces. A portrait of Sybil hung over the formal fireplace in which a fire had never been lighted. The logs of silver birch could have been hand-polished.

Van Sweringen came in presently, carrying a tray on which were glasses, brandy, Scotch and sherry. "May I mix you a drink, sir?"

"Thanks," Rye said. He looked at the tray. "Is that some of the special Amontillado?" It appeared that it was. He watched Van Sweringen pour it almost reverently. He wondered what butlers thought about, and why so few of them made first-class blackmailers. He wondered what Van Sweringen thought about him, William Rye. Holding the glass by its fragile stem he savored the fine old sherry appreciatively. "Gerald around, Van?"

"No, sir, Mr. Gerald didn't come home for dinner." Brown eyes that were like a self-respecting spaniel's, lids pouched a little with age, regarded Rye for a moment. "Mrs. Callahan is in. Shall I announce you?"

"Thanks."

An electric clock in a French enamel case made nine o'clock a musical interlude. As though this were her cue, Sybil Callahan accomplished a perfect stage entrance. She stood poised in the hall arch, three steps above Rye and apparently a little startled at seeing him there. "Why, William, why didn't they *tell* me?"

Rye got to his feet. "Always the gentleman," he said. "How are you, Sybil?"

She came down the steps, gracefully and with none of the provocative sway she sometimes used. Sybil was being the perfect lady tonight. Under the artificial light her hair looked like burnished silver. Her gown and slippers were pale green, without ornamentation. There was an almost virginal fragrance about the scent she wore. She came very close to Rye and her wide-set blue eyes searched his face. "Did you — was that true, what the papers said?"

"Unh-hunh."

She breathed a little sigh of relief and her eyes dropped. When she lifted them again there was curiosity and just the faintest touch of apprehension in them. "What did you do — to him?"

Rye's mouth said that he was amused. The amusement did not quite reach his eyes. "Nothing."

She put a hand on his arm, almost diffidently. "You don't like me, do you, Bill?"

"I could," he said. "If you were anybody's wife but Callahan's I could like you a lot."

Embarrassment stained her cheeks. "Did you see the — ?"

Rye nodded. "They weren't so bad." He moved away from her, a little afraid of his own emotions. "I wish you'd stay away from places where worms like Ambrose hang out."

"Why doesn't Ed divorce me?"

"Ed is a proud man, Sybil. In his way, I think he still loves you." Rye shrugged impatiently. "At least he doesn't want to admit to the world that he hasn't got what it takes to hold you."

Her mouth curved downward. "He has, if he'd put a little time in at it."

It occurred to Rye that this might be true or it might not. You never could tell about Sybil. It also occurred to him that if she really wanted a divorce, she could get it very easily with Carmelita Machado as a weapon. He decided that he would have to be very, very careful to keep them apart. "You saw the governor at dinner?"

"Yes."

"How does he feel about his re-election?"

"He's afraid Ed is losing some of his influence in the city administration. Granger's advertising seems to be have some effect." She moved gracefully across the room to the table with the tray on it. Apparently interested in the decanters she said, "Didn't I see you talking to some man in a car outside?"

Rye's stomach muscles quivered slightly. His face betrayed nothing of his surprise. "Just a guy I had hang around for a while. I thought Ambrose might show up and make trouble."

She seemed satisfied with the explanation. "He won't?"

"Not if he hasn't by now." He laughed a little. "There was always the possibility that he didn't keep all of his stock in trade in one place."

Van Sweringen appeared in the hall archway. "Telephone, madame."

"I'll take it in my room." She looked at Rye. "Excuse me, Bill?"

"Sure." He wondered if it was Harris Friedlander calling. For a man who was Callahan's attorney and allegedly one of his friends, Friedlander had been acting kind of funny lately. It was possible that this was entirely because of Sybil.

Van Sweringen stood aside for Sybil to pass. Then, as though at an afterthought, he came down the steps and across to where Rye stood at the tall windows. "Pardon me, sir, there was a lady telephoned for Mr. Gerald. She seemed quite put out that he had failed to keep an appointment with her."

Rye watched his cigar make a smoke ring all by itself. He thought that life was like that. Maybe if you didn't try so hard, if you just went away somewhere — say to a tropical island with a girl like Sheridan McKay — things would work out. He did not look at Van Sweringen. "Annoyed, was she?"

"Very."

"Happen to leave her name?"

Van Sweringen lowered his eyes. "A Miss Dee, I believe, sir. Miss Blossom Dee."

"Know who she is, Van?"

"Yes, sir," Van Sweringen said. He was very apologetic about the whole thing. "That is, I understand she — ah — sings at one of Mr. Powers' clubs."

"I like the way you put it," Rye said. "So genteel." He still did not look at Van Sweringen's face. "If Mr. Gerald happens to come home you might just forget to mention that Miss Dee called."

"Very good, sir." Van Sweringen went away.

It was perhaps five minutes after that when Callahan and Governor John Charles Quarrie came down the hall. Callahan had his arm around the governor's shoulders. He saw Rye standing there in the middle of the living room and detoured his distinguished guest down the three steps. "You know Rye, John."

The governor nodded. "Mr. Rye." His voice was a pleasant barytone. He was as handsome as Paul McNutt, and it was said that the women's vote never worried him. Rye neither liked nor disliked him. He just thought that Callahan felt about the governor the way that he, Rye, felt about Callahan, and that this was not always a good thing. He too nodded, not offering his hand. "You're looking well, Governor."

Quarrie smiled. "I've never seen you looking otherwise, Mr. Rye."

Callahan's laugh was too loud. "This is Ed Callahan's house you two are in. You'd think it was Mrs. Richbitch's lawn festival."

"The governor awes me," Rye said. This time the smile reached his eyes and stayed there. He put out his hand. "I guess we're both working for the same thing, sir."

"Maybe Edward will buy us a drink to seal the bargain," Quarrie agreed. After a while all three men lifted their glasses. "To better government."

"And cheaper," Rye said.

Callahan almost choked. "Remind me to cut your salary, will you?" He rang for Van Sweringen, who came in with the governor's coat and hat and stick. The trooper in the uniform of the State Guard stood at attention in the hall. "Well, good-night, John," Callahan said.

"Goodnight, Ed." Quarrie paused with a foot on the lower step and looked back over his shoulder. "Take care of him, Mr. Rye." He went out, a tall, very handsome gentleman with a state trooper at his back and an election facing him.

"A good guy," Callahan said.

Rye nodded and finished his drink. "A good guy."

Presently they went back along the hall to the library. This too was a big room, but the books and the deep leather chairs and the fire made it comfortable. Callahan's broad face was flushed and his eyes were a little resentful. "What are you doing in town? I thought — "

"That I was on my way to Mexico?"

"Yes."

Rye pretended to be reading some of the book titles. "The mountain and Mahomet," he said. "Mexico appears to have come to us."

Behind him there was a little tinkling crash. Callahan had dropped his glass. "You mean — ?"

"Yes." Turning, Rye discovered a look that was half fear, half something else in the older man's eyes. "I just ran into it by a fluke." In a voice that he made carefully devoid of inflection he recounted the meeting with Lou Small. He did not mention why he had thought Lou Small was someone else.

Callahan's spatulate fingers worried the bristly iron-gray mustache. When Rye was finished there was no sound at all for a little while. A log in the fireplace burned through and fell apart with a great crackling and shower of sparks. Rye stepped on one of the sparks. "I'd better handle this in my own way."

Callahan looked at him. "No." The fear was gone from his eyes now and there was nothing but anticipation in them. He looked younger.

"What do you mean, no?"

Callahan's voice was suddenly eager. "I want to see her."

"You're a fool."

"All right, then, I'm a fool." He began pacing the room, not heavily as he sometimes paced, but as though the years of soft living had fallen away from him. When presently he faced Rye directly he was the Ed Callahan who had bulled his way to the top of Calexico Oil, and almost to the top of the political heap. "I don't care how you handle it, but you'll handle it so I see her."

CHAPTER 5

THE pianist was someone who loved music. Depth and feeling more than made up for any lack of technical brilliance. You felt that whoever was playing, was playing by ear, and doing a better job of catching the writer's full meaning than a perfectionist. Presently a voice joined the piano, low and throaty and sweet. It was not until later that Rye learned that pianist and vocalist were one and the same. The song was *Estrellita*.

He stood in the shadow of the closed flower shop next door, inconspicuous but not furtive. He appeared to be just waiting for someone. His car was parked down the street a little ways. Up the block a neighborhood movie house disgorged another handful of customers. A street car came around the corner of Seventh Street and ground its way up the hill past Rye to Sixth. Some people got off and went into the all-night drugstore on the corner. *Estrellita* ended. But the memory, as they say, lingered on.

Presently Rye's cigarette described a glowing arc toward the gutter and he came out of the shadow and went up nine brownstone steps railed with wrought iron to the front door. The fanlight over the door was a stained glass edition of The Lord's Supper. Over the bell there was a framed sign that said: ROOMS. Rye rang the bell.

The woman who opened the door was scrupulously neat in stiff black. White tatting at her throat and wrists was her only concession to frivolity. She was a large, full-breasted woman, but not in the least militant. White hair which had never felt the shears and a labyrinth of tiny wrinkles suggested the reason for the faded look in her eyes. Rye was sorry he wasn't going to be able to rent a room from her. He felt that she would be disappointed. He took off his hat. "Pardon me, I'm looking for a Miss Machado."

"Oh."

It was as he had feared. She was disappointed. She didn't forget to be polite, though. She held the door wider. "Won't you come in? I'll tell her you're here." When he was safely inside she rustled toward closed double doors at the right, pausing at the threshold long enough to look back at him and ask, "What name shall I say?"

"Rye."

She thought that was a curious name. Her eyes and her lips struggled with it for a moment. Then, embarrassed, she slid the doors apart, hurried through and closed them after her. Rye sat on the extreme edge of a stiffly upholstered walnut settee and looked at himself in the mirror of a walnut hat rack which reminded him somehow of an octopus. For no reason at all except that there was probably a worn spot beneath it, a crocheted rug depicting a stag at bay lay diagonally between the parlour doors and the foot of carpeted stairs leading upward. Somewhere in the vague region above a muted radio relayed the ten o'clock news. Otherwise it was very quiet. It was so quiet that when the double doors parted again their rumble was like thunder. "Hello." It sounded a little like "Allo," though the accent was so vague as to be almost negligible. There was nothing vague about the girl herself. She was as vivid as a field of poinsettias at Christmas time. "You come from Mr.

Small, no? You have come for to talk business, yes?"

"Yes." With some difficulty Rye withdrew his eyes from the picture she made. Behind her the parlour was empty. The white-haired old lady had vanished, apparently by some other door. "May I come in?"

Eyes so very like Callahan's that it made his throat ache regarded Rye curiously. He imagined that after the shabbiness of Lou Small he was something of a contrast at that. The eyes were gray and direct and wise beyond their years. Hair as dark as midnight crowned a small proud head. Her skin had the golden warmth of apricots drying in the sun. "Yes." Without turning, still studying his face, she backed into the room and sat on the bench before the upright piano.

Rye came in, closing the doors behind him. He laid his hat carefully on a small table on which was an onyx reading lamp and a Gideon bible. He did not remove his topcoat. He looked at the piano. "Was that you I heard singing *Estrellita?*"

She nodded. "*Si.*" She changed that quickly to "Yes." She continued to watch his face.

"You're very good," Rye said.

Her shrug said that while this might be true it was relatively unimportant. "You 'ave find this man Callahan for me?"

Rye shook his head regretfully. "There are many Callahans in this city, chiquita." His use of the word brought a brighter flush to her cheeks. "It will take much time, I'm afraid." You could see how embarrassed he was to mention it, but after all business was business. "And time is money, no?"

She bit her lip. "But I have paid the money!"

"Ten dollars," Rye agreed. "That is for one day's work." He spread his hands. "But if in one day we have not found him — "

She was angry now. "Señor did not tell me that."

"He must have thought you understood it," Rye said. His eyes became bright and hard and intent. "If you tried any of the other agencies you must have realized that ten dollars was a ridiculous fee."

Her shoulders drooped, tiredly. It was only with great difficulty that Rye kept from going over and patting them. She was suddenly quite young, too young to be attempting whatever it was that she had in mind. Under his breath Rye cursed Callahan and his own silly allegiance to the man. He said, "You did try elsewhere, didn't you?"

"Yes."

Rye's breathing quickened a trifle. "Who?"

Not looking at him she named a couple of the larger agencies. She must have got them out of the phone book. "When they find I do not have much money they send me to Señor Small."

"You tell them what you wanted?"

"Only that I wish to find a man."

Rye was insistent. "But you did not name the man?"

She shivered, thought it was not cold in the room. "No."

He was relieved. He came and sat on the piano bench beside her. "Perhaps that is our trouble, chiquita. Perhaps if we knew a little more — if you were a little more frank with us about why you want to find this man — " His smile was insinuating without being an actual smirk. "If there is money involved we might be willing to work on a contingent basis."

The small hands in her lap became fists. "It is not a matter of money."

This time it was Rye who shivered. "A matter of hate, perhaps? Or revenge?"

She stood up quickly. "No!"

Rye turned and let his fingers trail idly over the keyboard. His face was lean and dark and a little cruel. "You have a passport, chiquita?"

Lithe as a cat she came to her feet and whirled on him. "W'y you ask me that?"

"We detectives have little ways of finding out about our clients," Rye said. He shook his head. "I'm afraid the immigration authorities are going to be very angry with you." He sighed. "They may even put you in jail."

Sudden terror turned her legs to jelly. When she would have fallen he put out an arm and drew her down beside him again. "Perhaps I can help you even yet, little one." Through his overcoat he could feel the trembling of her body. Her hair had the fragrance of temple incense. "Would you like me to help you?"

Blue-black lashes shadowed cheeks gone absolutely barren of color. After a long while she said in a voice scarcely above a whisper, "For — money?"

"Perhaps."

"But if I have none?"

His arm tightened about her. "This man you seek may be more fortunate." Comprehension dawned in her eyes, but there was no avarice. It was as though she saw through Rye, and beyond him, and he could almost feel her making up her mind that she must, of necessity, play it his way — at least up to a point. He remembered that they matured early in the tropics. He withdrew his arm about her waist. "Suppose I find this one for you, then what?"

She wouldn't look at him. "It is for you to say, Señor."

"You have some sort of a hold on him?"

Briefly her eyes lifted and he read in them the fury of a wounded jaguar. She was smart enough to mask it instantly. "If he is very rich, perhaps, or very important."

Her mother, she said, had been one of the finest singers in all of Mexico. Beautiful, too. But one did not sing so well with a broken heart, yes? There had been a period when there was no singing at all.

The word pictures came a little faster now. Brief interludes of prosperity when Carmel Machado secured engagements in the cafes. It was during one of these that she had met and married a man named El Segundo Ruiz. A small inheritance Carmel had received from a maternal grandfather may have influenced Ruiz to accept more or less philosophically a child that was not his own, but when the money was gone and Carmel could no longer support him in the style to which he was accustomed, things had got pretty bad. For Carmelita there had been sneers, and sometimes beatings, though these were as nothing compared to the leering suggestions when it turned out that she was to be as beautiful as her mother had been.

"Your mother ever try to get hold of this man Callahan?"

"No."

"Then maybe it wasn't all his fault," Rye said.

She looked at him. "Ees run way, don't he?"

"Before you were born."

She was too intent on her problem to notice that Rye seemed to know almost as much about the circumstances as she did. "For myself I do not care. Ees for what he does to my mother."

"She ever talk about him to you?"

"No." After a little while she added. "She is not want to hurt me, I think:"

"Then how did you find out?"

It appeared that Carmel had been a little feverish along toward the end. Also there were scraps of letters she had tried to write before accomplishing the one Callahan had actually received.

"Does Ruiz know?"

Fear crept back into the girl's eyes. "I can not say, Señor." She began to tremble all over again. "Think you these — these officers will find me?"

Rye hazarded a guess. "You're more afraid of Ruiz than you are of the immigration people, aren't you?" He had another flash of intuition. "It took money to get up here. Where'd you get it?"

She tried to speak, couldn't.

Rye drew a deep breath. "All right, we'd better get out of here. Go upstairs and pack your things." She didn't move. With some surprise he realized that she wasn't looking at him at all. She was looking at the doorway behind him and it was the paralysis of utter terror which kept her from screaming. He turned. The man was the fattest Mexican he had ever seen. Rolls of fat bulged over his low collar and hung down like turkey wattles. Fat, olive-brown cheeks pushed his eyes almost closed. Oddly enough he was not sloppy looking. Perhaps because of his very fatness there wasn't a wrinkle in his well-cut dark wool suit. He was disposed to be jovial. "So there you are, my little one!" Fatly, slyly, his voice crept around the room. "My little thief."

Rye said angrily, "So she's a thief, too." He took a step toward the fat man. "We didn't know that."

Heavy-lidded eyes opened a little wider. "We, Señor?"

"The Bureau of Immigration." He half turned and looked at the girl. Her eyes were fixed, like a sleepwalker's, on the fat man's face.

Her body was rigid. "Get your things, baby, we're going for a little ride."

With unbelievable rapidity the fat man produced a pistol from his pocket. "I do not know you, Señor, but of two things I am very sure. You are not of the Immigration, nor does the little one go for ride with you." His eyes crinkled and he laughed. "You see, I am listen for some little time outside the door." He gestured with the gun, gently. "Come, Carmelita."

"So you don't think I'm an officer," Rye said. He put two fingers between his lips and whistled shrilly. "I guess that'll show you." He watched surprise, then doubt come into the fat man's eyes. Upstairs, feet began moving around, and at the same instant someone started up the stone steps outside. The fat man's pistol steadied on Rye's middle. "You will to stand perfectly still, please." He backed through the double doors and slammed them shut. In the hall a woman screamed and there was the sound of a blow. Rye saw Carmelita sway, caught her and placed her carefully in a chair. He was quite sure that by this time the fat man had gotten safely away; safely, at least, for William Rye. The fat man had a pistol. He opened the hall doors and looked out. A buxom blonde with her hat slightly askew was weaving drunkenly about on her knees as though looking for something. On the stairs two or three people were staring at her, fascinated. Rye addressed the blonde: "What happened?"

"Someone hit me!"

"Who?"

She was outraged. "How do I know? A guy." She straightened her hat and with some difficulty got her eyes into focus on Rye's face. "A fat guy."

Rye's tongue and teeth made disapproving sounds. "Apparently no gentleman," he said. He backed into the parlor and closed the doors.

CHAPTER 6

SALMON and gold and blue chintz made the room bright and warm and lived in. The bellhop finished fiddling with the windows and the Venetian blinds and the drapes, and carefully avoiding Rye's eye asked if there would be anything else, sir. Rye said no, he didn't think so, and gave him a half dollar and watched him depart. Carmelita came back from exploring the adjoining bedroom and bath. She seemed to have marvelous recuperative powers. For one who less than forty minutes ago had had to be resuscitated from a dead faint she looked pretty good. The alleged fur collar of a fifteen-dollar department store coat framed her small triangular face and heightened the color in her cheeks. Gray eyes were a little tragic but no longer afraid.

"Why you do this for me?" Her gesture approved of the Commodore's best ten-dollar suite.

"Don't let Lou Small's shabby office fool you," Rye said. "We can afford to treat a client right. A profitable client."

She seemed a little disappointed.

"Besides," Rye said with every evidence of sincerity, "I like you." He crossed to the windows and stood looking down at people coming along the lighted forecourt. "Besides, if the Callahan thing fizzles out, I think I can find a spot for that voice of yours."

"But what of Ruiz?"

"I'll take care of El Segundo," he said. He thought a little about the fat man and the fat man's pistol. He thought that he had handled the situation very well, considering.

Carmelita's voice was low. "You were very brave, Señor."

Rye shook his head. "You wouldn't be any good to him dead. And shooting me would have involved no end of trouble." He shrugged. "He'll be around later."

She was startled. "Here?"

"No. He'll look me up to find where I've got you."

She came a step towards him, her eyes gone suddenly wide and dark. "And then you will to kill him?"

"Maybe," Rye said. He had no intention of killing Mr. El Segundo Ruiz unless the fat man made it absolutely necessary. He put on his hat. "How much money have you?"

It developed that she had less than twenty dollars. Rye considered giving her some more, decided against it. "All right, anything you want you can get at the shops downstairs. Just have 'em put it on the bill." He went to the door.

She caught her breath. "Then you do not want — you will not stay with Carmelita?"

Rye looked at her. "Don't think I don't want to," he said earnestly. He came back and put a firm brown hand under her chin. "You're very beautiful, chiquita, but for a while I think we'd better keep this strictly business." He went out rather hurriedly.

Down in the lobby a dapper young man with a pink cherub's face and wise eyes was pretending to read a newspaper. He spoke from a mouth corner. "Some babe." His name was Earl Holly and he was a private detective.

"Keep an eye on her," Rye said.

Holly leered. "For her sake or yours?"

"Both, maybe," Rye said. He looked at the people in the lobby. He didn't see any of the hotel detectives. The clock over the mail clerk's desk said that it was 11:25. "If she goes out or makes any phone calls I'd like to know about it." He appeared to be reading the headlines over Holly's shoulder. "When she was packing I think I saw her put a pistol in her bag."

"She probably thought she'd have to fight you off."

"Probably," Rye agreed. Music came out of the supper room, and laughter and the sound of dancing feet. The bell captain in his waist-high booth looked like a tired jockey after a hard race. Rye went down curving carpeted stairs to the cocktail lounge where he had a glass of straight seltzer. After a while he entered a phone booth and called Callahan. "Well, I've seen her."

Callahan's voice was eager. "Was she — Do you think she's — ?"

"Like you?" Rye pretended to consider that. "Well, she hasn't a mustache." He listened to Callahan's cursing for a moment. "Could be. I don't know yet."

"I'll take a look at her myself."

"No."

Callahan's voice got an edge to it. "We've been together a long time, Bill. I don't like that very well."

"Listen," Rye said passionately, "nothing has changed since this morning — except for the worse. You were afraid it might be a trap, remember? You thought it might be one of Granger's tricks." Under straight black brows his eyes were hard and bright. "You keep on acting like a kid about this and you're going to pull everything out in the open."

Callahan was still angry. "What do you mean, for the worse?"

"The lady's carrying a gun," Rye said.

"For me?" Callahan laughed.

"You think it isn't?" Rye demanded. "She wants to use it on you so bad she was willing to steal the money to get it, and to get up here. She's willing to pretend to fall in with a blackmailing scheme, or to sleep with me if necessary, just so I finger you for her."

Callahan was amused. "You don't say!"

"Here's something else that's screamingly funny," Rye said. "The money she stole belonged to a man named El Segundo Ruiz. Remember him? Her step-papa. Maybe he just wants his money back; maybe he thinks she can earn him a nice living, but ten will get you fifty he wants her to use on you."

"You mean Ruiz is up here too?"

"Also with a gun," Rye said. He described his meeting with the fat man. "I've arranged it so he can find me under more advantageous circumstances." His laugh was without humor. "More advantageous to me." He hung up.

A man came out of a door marked "Gentlemen," saw Rye, nodded, moved with ponderous dignity toward a booth in which were two other men and three women, thought better of it and returned to take the just vacated stool at Rye's left. "Mr. Rye, isn't it?" His voice was full and rich and mellow. You felt that here was a man literally bursting with the milk of human kindness, just like his publicity man said. All you had to do to get a free meal at any of Weldon Granger's cafeterias was to go there and tell 'em you didn't have any money. Rye had never seen anybody actually do this, but he'd heard that it was a fact. Advertised properly it had made a great hit with the Thirty-Dollars-Every-Thursday vote. It had even elected a Granger-sponsored district attorney and mayor. Rye politely admitted his identity. "Have a drink?"

"Well, ah — hmmm — I believe I will." Granger's paunch pushed his dress shirt against the bar. Large pink hands rested squarely on it, indicating a man about to make a momentous decision. He ordered buttermilk and soda.

Rye regarded him with a kind of horror. "Is that good?"

"Very good," Granger assured him. He smacked his full, cherry-red lips. "Excellent." In the black-bar mirror his pale gold eyes examined Rye cautiously. "Yours must be a trying job at times, Mr. Rye."

"You've no idea," Rye agreed.

Mr. Granger cleared his throat. "I realize that that is part of our modern vernacular, but it is not quite a fact. The truth is — well, I do have some idea." He set his glass down carefully. "Must keep you pretty busy — the Callahan family being what it is."

"Oh, it does," Rye said. "They're nothing but a bunch of heels." Self-pity almost overcame him. "The things I could tell you — "

Suspicion darkened the pale blue eyes. "You wouldn't be — ah — ribbing me, would you, Mr. Rye?"

Rye was indignant. "Who, me?"

"No matter," Mr. Granger said hastily. "It just occurred to me that for a sum — a very tidy sum, I might add — you could be induced to come over into our camp."

Rye looked at him. "Would I get free meals at your cafeterias?"

Granger's plump pink face became a shade darker. "Now you are joking me." He seized his glass and emptied it. "Perhaps I put it a trifle badly, but I am a blunt man, Mr. Rye. If I may say so, a four-square man."

"You don't have to tell me," Rye said. "I read the Post-Express." With every appearance of relish he drank the last of the Scotch-diluted soda. "Just what would you consider a tidy sum?"

Granger patted his full lips with a pristine handkerchief. "That would depend on the quality of the information." For the first time he looked directly into Rye's eyes. "Say ten thousand? Fifteen?"

"You under-estimate me."

"All right, twenty-five, then."

Sybil Callahan came down the curving stairs on the arm of Harris Friedlander. They made a striking couple. Her blue eyes widened at sight of Rye and his companion, and Rye expected a rather bad half hour with Callahan the next day. Sybil would like nothing better than a rift between her husband and his confidential agent. Friedlander nodded pleasantly enough and piloted the lady into a booth. Rye wondered how much it would be worth to Weldon Granger, or to Sybil Callahan, for that matter, to know about a certain young lady up in Room 722. He looked at Granger. "I'll have to think it over for a day or two."

Granger stood up. "That will be quite all right, Mr. Rye. Quite." He smoothed the dress coat over his hips. "Thank you for the drink." He and his dignity moved ponderously down the crowded aisle and presently was lost to sight.

Rye went home. As he was crossing the lobby to the elevators a lady stood up in his path. "You son of a bitch," she said loudly. The night clerk and the elevator boy and half a dozen residents cranked their necks. Blossom Dee appreciated their interest. "You son of a bitch," she repeated. She was very drunk.

Rye took off his hat. "Hello, Blossom." With apparent carelessness he laid a hand on her arm. He hoped his fingers would leave good deep bruises. "Now that you've told everybody what I am, maybe you'd like to tell me why you think so — privately."

She attempted to kick him in the shins. "You let me go, you — " Whatever she had intended calling him this time was lost to posterity as Rye put an arm around her waist, his hand pressing her ungirdled diaphragm, hard, shutting off her wind. Her face turned a kind of sickly green beneath the make-up.

Rye spoke to his audience. "You'll have to excuse us. The lady is a little upset." The lady was more than a little upset. She was paralyzed in the crook of his arm. Her heels were a good half inch off the floor when Rye entered the elevator. "Hurry it up, Skeets." The car ascended swiftly, Skeets pretending that it took great concentration to run it. Once inside his own apartment Rye's embrace became a trifle less intimate. "You ought to give up liquor except in a small way, Blossom. It makes you say things you shouldn't."

Miss Dee was too busy to argue even that. Fish-like her mouth gulped air into starved lungs and presently it became evident that she was going to be sick. Rye carried her into the bathroom, sat her on a bath stool and pointed her face in the right direction. "It's your struggle from now on," he said. He went out, closing the door delicately behind him. His nostrils were flared and a little white.

A moment later Blossom Dee was standing in the bedroom doorway. She was a medium tall girl with green eyes and blue-black hair cut long and done in a roll at the base of her neck. Her Labrador mink coat was open, disclosing a gown of gold lamé. Her too-red mouth was smudged, as though she might have wiped it on the back of a hand. Rye crushed out his cigarette.

"Feeling better, Blossom?"

"No."

Rye reached for the phone. "Then maybe I'd better call up Powers and have him come and get you."

She crossed the room with the undulant grace of a stripper. "Think you're smart, don't you?"

"Not particularly."

Her mouth was sullen. "What does a lady have to do to get a drink around here?"

"Just be reasonable," Rye said. He went out to the kitchenette, which someone had thoughtfully straightened up in his absence. He was squeezing limes into tall frosted glasses when she came and stood in the door, watching him. He saw that she had discovered her mouth was on crooked and fixed it. "I suppose Gerald wanted to know if there was any truth in the Pat Powers-Blossom Dee story?"

"We'd have been married tonight if you hadn't had to shoot off your face."

"That's the trouble with me," Rye said amiably. "My nose is too big." He poured some Irish whisky on top of the lime juice and squirted seltzer down the inside of the glasses. "Would that have been smart — marrying him? Gerald hasn't got a dime except his allowance, and Callahan can stop that any time he feels like it."

"We'd have gotten by."

Something in her tone surprised him into looking at her. He was still more surprised to find two very large, very moist tears hovering on her lower lashes. "Don't tell me you — "

"I — I kind of like the guy," she admitted. She fumbled in her bag for a handkerchief, couldn't find one, accepted one of Rye's and blew her nose angrily. "You wouldn't understand that, of course, me being what I am." After a while she picked up her glass and carried it into the living room. "If it'll do you any good, I'm sorry I blew my top downstairs."

"Forget it." Rye straddled a straight chair, balancing his drink on the back of it. "I've nothing against you personally, Blossom. It's just that I've got to look out for Callahan." He sipped at the edge of his glass. "Say you married Gerald; say you just went on, not marrying him, and got caught at it. Either way, Powers would be sore, and there'd be a stink." From the corner of his eye he watched her face. "Pat is a bad man to have sore at you, Blossom."

Involuntarily she shivered. "I suppose so."

"Why don't you try breaking with him first?" Rye suggested. "Break it off clean, and stay away from Gerald. Then, after six months or so, if you still feel the same way, and Gerald does, I'll help you."

Sea green eyes lifted to his. "You mean that?"

"As nearly as I ever mean anything." He got up and began moving a trifle aimlessly about the room. "What did Gerald say to you?"

Her mouth drooped. "The usual thing, I guess. I'd have told him about Pat, only I thought he knew. I thought everybody knew." She lifted her glass and drank thirstily. "Anyway, one thing led to another and I finally kicked him out and got tight. And the tighter I got, the more I thought about you, and so — " She flushed.

"Forget it," he said again. His eyes were amused rather than angry. "I'd probably have done the same thing myself." He stiffened as someone knocked on the door. Behind his back his right hand opened the shallow drawer in a wall console. There was a gun in the drawer. "Come in."

He felt just a little silly when his newest visitor turned out to be neither Pat Powers nor El Segundo Ruiz. It was Miss Sheridan McKay. She was, he thought, quite lovely in spite of her surprise

Dig Me A Grave

and a certain amount of justifiable displeasure at finding him entertaining another woman. "Hello, Sherry." He was constrained to perform a rather stilted introduction. "Miss Dee — Miss McKay." He carefully closed the drawer with the gun in it.

They measured each other. Finally they both said how happy they were, and Sherry said, looking at Rye, "I'm sorry, I just happened to be passing and saw your lights," and Blossom, yawning frankly but falsely, got up and moved her provocative body toward the door. "Well, I think I'll be toddling along."

"Oh no, it's I who should be going," Sherry said, and Blossom said, "No, really, I was just going anyway." With her hand on the knob she turned and looked at Rye. "Maybe I'll try it the way you suggested." She went out.

Miss McKay made rather too obvious a point of looking in the bedroom. Rye regarded her quizzically. "Find anything incriminating, darling?"

Completely unembarrassed she gave him a level stare. "Just what is it she is going to try the way you suggested?"

"There you go," Rye complained. "Always reading double meanings into things." Melting ice cubes had diluted his drink to the point where it was no longer palatable. He drank it anyway. "We were discussing painted toenails and she said hers peeled, and I said mine never did, because I tied 'em on with string, and — " He smiled at her. "Jealous, pet?"

"A little," she confessed.

Rye touched her hair with his lips. "Well, may there be just a little bit in me too." For the first time in twenty-four hours he laughed as though he actually meant it.

The telephone rang. Rye considered letting it ring, but was finally impelled to answer it. "Yes?"

"Bill? Earl Holly."

The tiny muscle at the corner of Rye's mouth began to twitch. "What happened?"

"She got away from me, Bill." Holly sounded like a hundred-yard man who has just done a mile. "Christ, that babe can run like a deer!"

"So you chased her," Rye said.

"Well, sure, but — "

Rye smothered the impulse to curse. "All right, pal, forget it. Go back and sit down. Maybe — She take any of her things with her?"

"No."

"Then maybe she'll have to come back to change her pretties one of these days." He replaced the phone and regarded Sherry McKay with disillusioned eyes. "It's been a trying day, darling. Could I just put my face down in your lap and cry?"

CHAPTER 7

SOME men were putting up a canvas banner across the face of the building opposite. "Now Let's Clean Up The State," it said, and: "Special Interests Must Go!" The inference was that the city and county had already been cleaned up. A lot of people were watching the workmen, craning their necks far back, and inside the plate glass windows of Granger's Cafeteria No. 1, a lot of people waiting for tables were watching the people on the sidewalk. The face of the traffic cop on the corner glistened butter-yellow in the Noon sun.

Behind Rye's back a newspaper rattled. The headlines were concerned with the war, as usual, making the death of one man, even by violence, of not much consequence. Lou Small rated less than a column, and part of that had been carried over to Page 2. "An unimportant little man," Rye said. "A shabby little man, in a shabby business." He turned and looked at Callahan. "Somebody is going to hang higher than a kite for killing him."

Callahan ran a thick forefinger around the inside of his collar. "They don't hang in this state any more."

"I'd forgotten," Rye said. He studied the carefully kept nails on his left hand. "Sometimes I think the horrors of the gas chamber ought to be better publicized. Hanging used to mean something to potential murderers." His smile did not quite reach his eyes. "Kind of a deterrent."

Callahan thrust his chair violently backward. "Damn it, you

don't for one lousy moment think I — "

"No," Rye said, "why should I?" After a while he said, "Probably a lot of people smoke the same kind of cigars you do." The tiny crumpled ball of cellophane on the desk lay like a stone wall between them. He smoothed it out into a long slender envelope. "I can see the defense attorneys telling the jury how generous you always were with your private brand."

Callahan's eyes had pouches under them. "Where'd you get it?"

"In the entryway leading up to Small's office." Rye shrugged his shoulders impatiently. "The cops found my phone number among Small's effects, so they took me down there to confront me with the body."

"And you picked the wrapper up right under their noses?"

"Yes."

For a moment Callahan's body was shaken as though by a strong wind. When he finally spoke his voice was sullen. "All right, I was there, but I didn't kill him. He was already dead when I — "

Anger muddied Rye's eyes. "I told you you'd better let me handle this, Ed. I told you it was going to be dynamite." His nostrils flared, his breathing uneven. "But no, you had to be cute. You couldn't wait for me to set the thing up right for you."

Callahan ran thick fingers through his shock of iron-gray hair. "How do I know you didn't kill him yourself?"

Rye laughed harshly. "You and Belarski ought to get along well together." Detective-lieutenant Nick Belarski was one of the cops that had gotten Rye out of bed. "You'd better tell me what happened, Ed." Lean brown fingers crumpled the tell-tale bit of cellophane, dropped it into a wastebasket. "Exactly what happened."

There was something oddly like Gerald in Callahan's embarrassment. Perhaps, Rye thought, that's the trouble; they're too much alike. Thirty years separate them, yet in some things the father is as adolescent as the son. He frequently found it difficult to reconcile Callahan's achievements with this peculiar quirk in his nature which made him go off at a tangent. Callahan said angrily, "All right, all right, I'm going to tell you. Don't stand there staring at me like a crucified St. Peter!" When Rye continued to stare at him he sought relief in the heavy bronze paper knife, bending it almost double, straightening it out again. He was a little vain of the strength of his hands. "That telephone call of yours sounded phoney as hell — all the heavy menace and one thing and another." From under beetling brows his eyes searched Rye's face briefly, returned to his hands. "You didn't want me to see the girl in the first place. I thought you were pulling a fast one. So I decided I'd have a look around this — this Lou Small's place, figuring — "

"That he might lead you to her where I wouldn't?"

"I told you you wouldn't understand how I felt about this," Callahan said. He drew a deep breath. "Well, so I argued it back and forth for maybe an hour or so before I went down there. It was a walk-up building, not many people around, and I thought I'd — well, just go up and see if there was a light. Maybe you'd be there, maybe the girl would." His heavy shoulders moved irritably. "I don't know just what I intended to do."

The ensuing silence gnawed at Rye's nerves. "All right, never mind what you intended to do. What did you do?"

Callahan moistened his lips. His voice was tight and dry, as though it too needed moistening. "There was a light — behind the door — and I thought I heard voices. Trying to hear what was being said I inadvertently leaned on the door, and the damned thing wasn't fastened. He was — it was just sitting there, leering at me, and blood all over the front of him and on the desk — "

"I saw him," Rye said. "You can skip that part." He began pacing the room, nervously. "You saw nobody else? Anybody see you?"

"No."

"You hadn't heard any shots?"

Callahan shook his head. "No."

"So what did you do next? Go downstairs and light a cigar, so that anybody that *might* have been around could get a good look at your face?"

Callahan stared at him with a mixture of anger and incredulity. "Sometimes I wonder if you aren't made of stone. Am I supposed to stumble over a dead body and just take it in my stride?"

"You aren't supposed to be within miles of any dead bodies," Rye said. "I'm the guy that does the stumbling, remember? That's what you hired me for." He crossed to the windows and looked down at the banner bellying in the breeze. "This'll be all Granger needs," he said gloomily.

"If it breaks," Callahan agreed. Now that he had unburdened his soul, his normally aggressive manner was in the ascendant. He came over and stood at Rye's elbow. "Any reason why it should?"

Rye was moved to sarcasm. "Oh, no, no reason at all. The cops are just going to laugh it off, and Carmelita and her step-papa are going to think you've got troubles enough, so they'll just not mention it and go home, and everything will be lovely."

"The cops didn't have anything on you, did they?"

Rye pointed. "Belarski's across the street trying to look like a window-shopper right now."

Callahan cursed. "Does that mean — ?"

"That they didn't believe my story? How do I know?" Rye thrust his hands deep into trouser pockets. "Belarski would like not to believe it, but until something else comes up he can't help himself. I accounted for the phone number by telling him Small had heard I sometimes hired a private eye, and called me to see if he couldn't get on the gravy train."

"Well, that ought to hold him."

"It won't," Rye said. "It won't hold Granger, or the girl, or Ruiz either. Or Sybil," he added presently. "The girl and Ruiz — at least the girl — can positively tie me up with Small. I was supposed to be his partner. And if Ruiz happened to be hanging around when Small went out to the Westlake address last night, trying to find out what I'd done with the girl, he might have tailed him." His brows drew down in a frown of annoyance. "It's just a little thing, what the cops have got so far, but it's an entering wedge. Granger will smell something and go to work on it, because from me to you, and from you to the governor there's an unbroken chain. Anything can happen."

Confronted with an actual emergency, Callahan could be as coldly analytical as the next man. "You mentioned Sybil."

Rye looked at him. "Sybil wouldn't mind seeing you hanged either. That's almost as final as divorce."

"I ought to change my will," Callahan growled. "I've been meaning to do it for some time. I'll call Harris in the morning."

"That won't get you anything in this instance. If Sybil found it out she'd just be vindictive instead of avaricious." Rye shook his head. "No, the thing we've got to know first is whether my fleet-footed little Carmelita is the right girl. If she isn't, I can handle it."

"And if she is?"

"Maybe I can still handle it. I don't know. I'm making some guarded inquiries down in Mazatlan and Santa Caterina." He looked sidewise at Callahan's square florid face. "Meantime, if I could trust you not to do anything screwy I'd let you see her."

Callahan brightened. "How?"

"I'm going to take her to lunch," Rye said. By his watch he saw that it was almost one o'clock. "That is, if she hasn't given Holly the slip again." He put on his hat. "We'll be at Arnstein's about one-thirty. Don't stare at her."

Callahan flushed brick red. "I'm sorry about last night, Bill. I'll be good." An arm about Rye's shoulders he went to the door with him. "Who do you think did it — Lou Small, I mean?"

"Ruiz, probably. For a couple of other guesses, Carmelita and you." Unsmiling he watched the older man's skin turn a greenish brown. "The trouble is, we can't do much about it without bringing the whole thing into the open. Arresting either of the other two would pull you and Quarrie down as quick as though you'd done it yourself."

Again Callahan's fingers sought his throat. "But Christ, what motive could I have?"

"As good as the others," Rye said maliciously. "You all wanted some information you thought Small had." He opened the door and went out.

From her desk beside the anteroom's tall windows Sherry McKay admired the gray gabardine he was wearing. "Isn't that new?"

"Unh-hunh." Rye himself admired the cuffs on the trousers. "My tailor bootlegged them." He preened himself before the full-length mirror on the lavatory door. "In case anybody should ask you, my sweet, I really did take you home last night." He looked at her. "You might remember the exact time, too."

Her eyes had little golden flecks in them. "Someone interested in us? Or have you become interested in someone?"

"There was a slight case of murder the police would like to connect me with."

Ever so briefly her eyes closed, and two bright spots of color burned high up on her cheeks. "I've forgotten, are you supposed to have — ?"

Rye was shocked. "Oh, no, nothing like that!" He smoothed his tie. "Perhaps I stayed a little later than I should have. Say two-thirty?"

"But it was only — "

He nodded. "That's right, two-thirty. You remember because I made fun of the way your clock chimed the half hour." He went out and down to his car, pretending that he didn't see Lieutenant Nick Belarski getting into another one parked in a red zone down the street. It took him fifteen minutes to lose Belarski without looking as though he were trying to. When he entered the lobby of the Commodore his face was smooth and unworried.

He got into an elevator with some ladies and men who smelled nice and opulent and rode up to the seventh floor and presently was knocking at Carmelita's door.

She was in a beige wool skirt and short vacquero jacket over a frilly scarlet silk blouse. On her, the scarlet was not too vivid. Rye decided that she was just about the most beautiful thing he had seen, not excepting Miss Sheridan McKay. His voice was a caress. "Been lonely, chiquita?"

"A little," she confessed.

He thought of the shabby little man named Lou Small whom he had promised something he could not now pay. "Why did you go out, Carmelita?"

Her eyes grew dark and remote. "You would not understand these things, Señor Rye. Perhaps Carmelita, she is like the cat, that wild one who becomes restless at night and in strange places." Her smile was apologetic. "This city, it is so very big, no?"

"You did not by any chance go near the Señor Small?"

"No."

For the life of him he could not tell whether she was lying. It was almost inconceivable that anyone not a consummate actress could be so childishly naive one moment, so mature and seductive the next. He would have liked to look at her pistol, but decided to postpone that for the time being. He was already late for his appointment with Callahan. "There is a reason for my asking you that, chiquita. You are quite certain?"

"Of course."

"Then you will not go near him," Rye said. "You will not try to telephone him, nor admit to anyone that you ever knew him."

"But for why, Señor?"

He watched her face. "Because he was killed last night. Someone shot him."

Her reaction was unexpected. Though some of the color fled from her cheeks she did not cry out. "You think is me?"

"It was an idea," Rye said dryly.

She shook her head. "Is my father," she stated with great certainty. "Señor Small, he is find the right Callahan, but he is clumsy." She spread her small hands. "So he is killed." She stared at Rye with dawning suspicion. "But if he is know, then you must to know also." Quite suddenly she was a panting little hell-cat, beating at his chest with tiny furious fists. "Damn you, you play with Carmelita!"

He caught her wrists and held them. "It could have been Ruiz you know."

The breath went out of her in a gusty sigh. "Ahhh!" After a while she began to cry, not noisily but like a disappointed child. "Carmelita, she is little fool, no?" Her fingers curled into his lapels and she buried her face in the hollow under his chin. The perfume of her hair was like wine in his nostrils.

He said in a carefully repressed voice, "I can't have you going hysterical on me like this, chiquita. It is money we are after, not killing." He pushed her away from him. "If I find this Callahan for you and you kill him, then there is no money for me, and if there is no money, then why do I help you?"

She eyed him with a kind of stunned disbelief. "You do not feel, in here" — she patted the region over her heart — "the death of the little man who is your partner?"

"Perhaps," Rye said. He turned and again pretended to be interested in the view from the windows. "I have learned that there are better ways to hurt a man than by killing him, that's all."

He kissed her then, briefly, lest he forget himself entirely. In Spanish he said, "Fix your face, little one. After lunch there is a man for whom I would like you to sing *Estrellita*."

Arnstein's was crowded. Arnstein's was always crowded. It was getting so that it was almost as fashionable to be seen there as at the more popular Derbies, or Al Levy's, or even the Beverly-Wilshire, and the wise boys had formed the habit of dropping in at least once a day to pick up the dirt. Izzy Arnstein himself was known as a soft touch, and his floor shows were better than most because a lot of the topnotchers remembered the coffee and cakes he had staked them to when they weren't topnotchers. They were always glad to oblige with a little number between the soup and the entree.

Going in, you invariably had the feeling that you had suddenly been struck stone blind, especially in the daytime, but this soon passed and after a while you got so that you could even see as far as three tables away from you. The noise was terrific.

Rye watched Carmelita's face as the waiter brought them cocktails. "Like it?"

"Is horrible," she said. "Horrible but wonderful."

A spotlight began poking about the cavern, searching out celebrities, hovered for a full minute on Rye's table, finally passed on and impaled a musical star from one of the major studios. She was in the act of bawling out her waiter for spilling something down her neck, but she was a trouper too. When the orchestra swung into her current theme song she got up, wiped her mouth with a homey, cornfed gesture and gave out with all she had. The applause was deafening.

Rye's eyes came back from a study of the room to Carmelita's profile. "Think you could do that, little one?"

She was startled. "Now?"

"Oh, no," Rye said. He had located Callahan at last. The big man was at the end of the bar, staring across it at the girl's face. There was sweat on his forehead. Rye wondered how many of those about him who dealt in drama could appreciate this moment. He said in a matter-of-fact voice, "No, chiquita, not now. I'll have to speak to Izzy Arnstein first."

In a bare brick-walled room as unattractive as the backstage of a burlesque house Izzy Arnstein leaned on the battered grand piano and watched the girl's face. "Where'd you learn to sing like that, kid?"

"My mother."

"And where did *she* learn?"

Rye said, "Never mind that. We'll paint in the backdrop after you've made her famous." He looked at Carmelita. "Tired, hon?" She had sung three songs for Arnstein. It was four o'clock.

"Not very."

Arnstein was a small untidy man with shoe-button eyes and the nervous energy of Cantor. "She's different," he admitted. "No Miranda, but good. If she's got some clothes I'll spot her in the show tonight."

In the car again, tooling it leisurely through thickening traffic, Rye could feel her questing eyes on his face. Presently she said, very low, "Did I then do so badly, amigo?"

He turned and smiled at her. "That is much nicer than the 'Señor,' chiquita." He answered her question. "No, you were perfect." He wished her eyes were not so much like Callahan's. He wished he were in China, or even in Washington, D. C. A fog was beginning to drift in from the ocean, veiling a burnt-orange sun with silver gauze. "If you hadn't been, Izzy would have said you were swell, but he just didn't have an opening."

CHAPTER 8

THERE were some wires for Rye at the desk. They didn't tell him anything he didn't know. A parish priest in Santa Caterina had administered the last sacraments to a woman named Mrs. Carmel Ruiz. It was believed that she had had a daughter. Her husband, El Segundo Ruiz, had occasionally been in trouble with El Policia, but it seemed that he had friends and nothing ever came of it. Both husband and daughter had temporarily disappeared.

Rye went into the janitor's closet under the stairs, touched a match to the telegrams and watched them curl into black ash in the porcelain tub. He flushed the ashes down the drain.

There were a few people in the lobby, not many. Aside from the clerk and the elevator boy Rye didn't know any of them. He went up to his own apartment. There was a man sitting on the davenport, facing the door. All the drapes had been drawn and the lights were on. There was another man, standing in the opening to the kitchenette, picking his teeth. He looked at Rye without much interest, said, "Hiyuh, pal," examined the end of the toothpick, found nothing on it and tried again.

Rye just stood there for a moment, breathing gently through his nose. The man on the davenport was sitting upright, hands flat on his knees, like a deacon in church, only he did not look like a deacon. Behind the marble railing of a bank officers' enclosure he might have looked like a banker; behind a desk in Washington he might have been one of the better-known dollar-a-year men. But he certainly did not look like a deacon. Thinning sandy hair was parted neatly in the exact center and brushed smoothly back on either side of the rather too large but well-shaped head. His skin had a not unhealthy pallor, suggesting an unfamiliarity with the sun. His eyes had all the warmth of chrome plate. His name was Patterson Powers. "Come in and close the door, Rye."

Rye shook his head. "No, thanks, I don't mind the neighbors hearing us." He smiled at the gorilla with the toothpick. "You find everything you wanted in the refrigerator?"

"Oh, a smoothie." The hulk removed one of its shoulders from its resting place against the door jamb. "I don't like smoothies." A large foot took a tentative step in Rye's direction.

"Joe," Powers said. He did not raise his voice.

Joe returned to his original position. Renewed excavations with the toothpick finally brought something to light that looked like a gold filling. He regarded it with an air of pleased surprised. "Well what do you know about that!"

"Your dentist ought to love it," Rye said. Behind him in the corridor some people got out of the elevator. His eyes considered Powers. "I could have you thrown out, you know." And when Powers didn't register any apprehension: "Or maybe arrested for breaking and entering."

"Let's not talk about the law," Powers said quietly. "Not just yet." His mouth looked as though it had never smiled. "Where's Blossom?"

Rye's face expressed astonishment. "Blossom?"

"You heard me. I want her."

"I certainly can't blame you for that," Rye said. "The point is, why tell me about it?" Ignoring his former assertion that he had no secrets from his neighbors, and just to show that he wasn't afraid of Joe after all, he came in and shut the door and began taking off his coat and hat. "Why bring a punk like Joe along?"

"I happen to know that she was here last night."

"That's right," Rye said. He wondered how long Powers had been having the lady tailed. "I had a chaperon, and the chaperon will be a witness that Miss Dee left here of her own free will and all in one piece." In a wall mirror he examined his face to see if he needed a shave. He decided he did. "She was pretty drunk," he said casually. "Maybe she just went somewhere to sleep it off."

They could have been discussing an abstract problem for all the emotion that showed. Only Joe appeared really interested. His small bright eyes shuttled from one man to the other like a tennis fan following the ball. Powers looked at the tips of his black shoes. "And maybe she went somewhere with Gerald Callahan."

Rye turned then and leaned against the console under the mirror. "You ask him?"

"I can't find him," Powers said. "I'm asking you."

Rye made up his mind. "You and I have always got along pretty well, Pat. I don't want any trouble — not your kind of trouble — so I'm going to give you what I know." From the tail of his eye he watched Joe, because it was obvious that Joe was becoming a trifle restless. "Blossom sheds enough glamour for three women, and Gerald is nothing but an impressionable college punk." He drew a slow breath. "So I happened to see them together once and I warned him off. He told her about it, and she dropped by to suggest that I mind my own business." He began taking off his shirt. "I don't think she was really interested. She just had too big a load to carry all by herself, so some of it slopped over on me." He spread his hands. "Okay?"

"No."

"Why not?"

"Because I've got to see her, or him, before I'm satisfied." Powers got to his feet. "I don't care which one you find first."

Rye's mouth got a stubborn twist to it. "What's the matter with your own bloodhounds?"

"They lost her."

Rye looked at the hulk in the kitchen doorway. "If they're all like Joe, here, I can understand that." He opened the drawer behind him and took out the gun. "Your hands bother me, Joe. Don't make me pin 'em to your chest."

Joe pretended that his arms ended at the elbows. "I'll remember that, pally. I got a good memory for faces."

Pat Powers took up his hat. He was not wearing a topcoat, though the evening had turned chill. "There's a thought in that, Rye. It might be wise for you to locate the kid for me — or Blossom."

"And if I don't?"

With his hand on the door knob Powers paused and looked back. He had a capacity for utter quiet that was infinitely more menacing than the bluster of most men. "If you don't, Joe and some of the other boys will be around to see why not."

Joe spat deliberately in the middle of the rose-taupe carpet. "Yeah."

They went out.

A single drop of sweat formed under Rye's left armpit and ran down along his ribs. It was as cold as ice.

The telephone rang. Rye stared a little frightenedly at the gun in his hand, decided that it looked pretty silly there, put it back in the drawer and wiped his hands a trifle absently on his shirt. The phone continued to ring. He went over and answered it: "Dr. Snopleklauser speaking."

It was Callahan. "Quit clowning, will you?"

A silence ensued, a silence in which Callahan must have sensed Rye's disapproval, for abruptly he changed the subject. "She's the image of her mother, Bill."

"I gathered that," Rye said. "I saw your face."

"You want to take her in your arms and tell her you're sorry, and if she'll only forgive you and be willing to live quietly in a nunnery, or in some pent-house like a kept woman — "

"God damn you, stop it!"

"That's what you want, isn't it?" Rye persisted. He drew a deep breath. "Well, you can't have it, Ed. Maybe I'll try for it, maybe not, but offhand I'd say that it's the one thing in the state that you can't have. Not even if you wreck everything else to get it." He cradled the phone and went into the bedroom and began taking off the rest of his clothes.

Emerging from the shower some few minutes later, he laid out fresh shirt and shorts and was in the act of choosing between two dinner jackets when someone rang the doorbell. In a terrycloth robe and leather slippers he went into the living room, though he did not immediately unlock the door. His dark skin had a fresh, well-scrubbed look. "Yes?"

A voice on the other side of the door said its owner was Lieutenant Belarski. Rye got the impression that Belarski was not alone, and when he finally let the lieutenant in he saw that this was a fact. There was another dick. At least the presumption was that he was a dick, though to all intents and purposes he could have been the twin brother of Pat Powers' gorilla, Joe. It seemed that everybody was equipped with bodyguards tonight; everybody but William Rye. He wondered if he shouldn't do something about that.

Belarski looked significantly at the bedroom door. "All alone?" He was a sallow dark man nagged by acid indigestion and the knowledge that younger men had gone farther.

Rye said that he was all alone. "That is, practically." He watched the hefty detective get the nod from Belarski and lumber through the apartment making sure that Rye was telling the truth. "Fortunate, isn't it? Some day you guys are going to barge right in on somebody taking a bath."

Belarski's thin mouth curved downward. "Will we be embarrassed!"

Rye didn't even bother to pull the moth-eaten gag about a search warrant. "Maybe if you told me what you're looking for I could help you. But, of course, you're too damn tough for that."

"A guy got killed last night," Belarski said. "Remember?"

Rye nodded. "A lot of guys are getting killed."

Hefty closed the refrigerator door with a bang. "Ain't that a fact?" He shook his head sadly, expressing disapproval of violence. "This guy we're talking about wasn't much of a loss to anybody, far as we can make out, but we got our job to do, so we do it."

"Shut up," Belarski said, not angrily but as though he was just tired of hearing the big fellow talk. His turned down hat brim threw the upper half of his face in shadow. "We haven't crossed you off our list yet," he told Rye in a flat, emotionless voice. "Where were you all afternoon?"

"Out," Rye said.

"We know that." Belarski shrugged his narrow, well-tailored shoulders. "Well, let that pass for a while." He tilted his head back a little and Rye could see that the whites of his eyes were striated with delicate iodine traceries. The pupils were sharply defined, brilliant. "We're looking for a girl that might have knocked him off."

Rye was afraid that if he didn't move, didn't do something, it would look too much like an act. He was afraid that if he did he'd overdo it. The muscles of his stomach felt as though somebody had tied them in a hard knot. "Is that what your boy friend was looking for in the refrigerator?"

Hefty pretended that he thought this was very funny. "Jesus, you're a card." He appealed to Belarski. "Ain't he a card, Nick?"

"Shut up," Belarski said again. This time his voice had an edge. "Seen tonight's papers, Mister Rye?"

"No."

Belarski took one from his overcoat pocket and held it out. His eyes never left Rye's face. Rye saw that the paper was Granger's *Post-Express*, but he had no doubt that the other sheets were carrying the same banner: MYSTERY GIRL SOUGHT IN DETECTIVE SLAYING!

There was a pretty good picture of Lou Small. There was a fairly accurate description of Carmelita. It seemed that a couple of the better-known detective agencies had remembered referring a girl to Small. Righteously they had turned their information over to the police. Rye wondered if Carmelita's ex-landlady would recognize the description and be as helpful; he wondered if Small had actually called at the house.

"Funny thing," Belarski said. "There was no record of any such client in Small's office."

Rye felt that he could trust his own voice now. "Maybe she never went there."

"Or maybe someone else did and took the record away."

Rye's eyes grew bright and hard. "Meaning me?" He moved a little to one side, so that Belarski was between himself and Hefty. He had no illusions about cops. He had been one. "Listen, Nick, if you think you've got anything on me, get it over with. If you haven't, you ought to know better than expect me to break down and confess."

"Small had your phone number written down," Belarski said stubbornly. "The laboratory report shows it was written in the last day or two."

"I told you about that, Nick."

Belarski fumbled around in his pockets for a cigarette, finally got one alight. "Then you don't know any such girl?"

Rye watched Hefty sidling toward him. "No."

"It would go easier if you told us about it now than if we found out different and had to ask you later." Belarski waved almost negligently at the newspaper. "Somebody's going to find her for us."

Rye thought it quite probable. He thought it so very probable that the insides of his eyelids burned with the effort to keep his stare angry but unworried. The palms of his hands were sweaty. "I wish you luck, Nick."

Belarski jerked his head at his partner. "All right, let's get the hell out of here." They went out.

After a while Rye picked up the paper and turned to the editorial page. In a column headed: "Between The Lines" he found the item responsible for Belarski's second visit. "Can it be possible," the Granger-inspired writer inquired, "that William Rye, Edward Callahan's Number One Boy, knows more than he is telling about the **Lou Small case?"**

CHAPTER 9

IN his car again and passing through Civic Center on his way across town he was a little sorry that he had no ready substitute for the Carmelita who had stayed in a rooming house facing Westlake Park. Nor was he entirely complacent about the device he was using on the police to remove suspicion from himself in the matter of Lou Small's killing. But there was still the danger of Mrs. Kampf, Carmelita's ex-landlady, or one of the other roomers, recognizing the broadcast description in association with Small's murder. Mrs. Kampf had been willing to aid Rye to the extent of giving his name in case El Segundo Ruiz should return to inquire, but she was not the type to condone or abet murder. Rye wondered if she had just missed seeing the papers, or if, seeing them, the possibilities had escaped her. He wondered if Carmelita had seen the squib in the *Post-Express*. He tried to recall a time when so much had hung suspended on so slender a thread. He could not.

Sighing a little, Rye parked on Sixth Street, around the corner from Alvardo, and buttoning his top coat over his white shirtfront to make him less conspicuous, walked down the hill. A yellow street car clanked past him. White faces looked out of its lighted windows. Beyond it, fog swirled in the streets of the park and blanketed the lake. There was practically no traffic across the Wilshire causeway.

A man and a woman came out of the door whose fanlight was a stained-glass Lord's Supper. They turned in the direction of the neighborhood movie house. Behind them the door did not quite close, and yellow light came out of it, tinting the fog saffron. There was no sign of police lurking in the vicinity. Relieved, Rye went quickly up the stairs and into the lower hall with its walnut settee, its walnut, stag-antlered hatrack and the out-of-place throw rug which no doubt covered a worn spot in the carpet. Up above, a radio was playing, not noisily. Through open double doors Rye could see that the parlour was empty. He went down the hall to another door on which was a small porcelain plate: Manager. There was no answer to his knock. No sound except the casual radio upstairs.

He stood there a moment, debating whether he should go back and ring the front doorbell, or rouse some of the tenants or just wait. Presently it seemed to him that there was movement beyond the door and he rapped again, lightly. The sound continued, but still no one opened the door. Impatient now, he tried the knob, found that it turned under his hand and pushed the door in ahead of him. Light from the hall behind him made a broad yellow path in which his body was silhouetted against a figured carpet. The rest of the room was in pitch darkness. At the very end of the path of light was a hand. It was motionless.

His first conscious reaction was to take the handkerchief from his breast pocket and wipe the door knob he had just touched. There was that in the stillness of the wrinkled white hand which said it wasn't going to move again of its own volition, ever. Still using the handkerchief, he closed the door and snapped the latch. As his eyes became accustomed to the darkness he saw the outline of windows at the far end of the room. A faint breeze stirred one of the drawn shades and he recognized that as the sound he had heard from outside. He went over and pulled the sash down tight against the sill.

Someone knocked on the door. "Mrs. Kampf?"

Rye held his breath. Whoever was out there said, "She must have gone to church." Footsteps went away. The front door banged. Except for the radio upstairs it was very quiet again.

After a time he found the wall switch and turned the lights on. Mrs. Kampf had not gone to church.

On a cretonne-covered daybed her black silk dress looked oddly empty. Above the white tatting collar there were marks of fingers on her wrinkled throat. Her face was quite black.

CHAPTER 10

"I WAS afraid you'd stood me up again," Miss McKay said. She did not look like the kind of girl who is accustomed to being stood up.

In a gown of topaz, with slippers to match, and a Labrador mink coat she looked like something Percy Westmore had just turned out, ready to go on the set. The dark mahogany glints in her hair were rather pronounced tonight. Rye could not make up his mind about her eyes. He thought maybe it was the gown that made them look topaz instead of gray.

He helped her off with the coat and gave it to the check girl in Arnstein's foyer. "I resent that 'again.' It implies a certain instability on my part, whereas I am the most stable, the most trustworthy individual it has ever been my pleasure to meet." His dark face was smooth and untroubled.

With the coming of night, Arnstein's had lost its cavernous air. As usual it was crowded, but more sedately, and in the orchestra shell the men wore dinner jackets instead of just what they had happened to reach out and find on climbing out of bed. The place was well lighted.

A maitre came to the main arch and gave Rye the nod. They went in to a corner booth from which the dance floor and the bar were clearly visible. Patterson Powers was at the bar, talking with Izzy Arnstein. If Rye were surprised, or worried, his face gave no sign of it. He ordered cocktails, viewing Miss McKay with patent approval. "You wouldn't like to drive to Las Vegas tonight, would you?"

Her eyes crinkled at the corners. He thought that if she weren't very careful of it her nose might have freckles some day. "Are you suggesting that I become an honest woman, Mr. Rye?"

He thought of Sybil Callahan, who was supposed to be an honest woman. "Marriage would probably spoil you, at that."

"And you'd have to stay home, nights."

He nodded. "Or you wouldn't want to."

Bert Romero, the M.C., lifted the microphone down and carried it over to where some men were pushing a toy piano out on the floor. "And now, ladies and gentlemen, I give you *Estrellita* by none other than Estrellita herself!" He held out his hand and Carmelita came through the curtains, letting them fall behind her. There was a little applause, not much. Those of Arnstein's patrons who weren't sophisticated to the point of boredom liked to pretend they were.

She was even more vivid than Rye had remembered her. Older too, though this may have been the gown and the background. Without touching Romero's hand, almost as though she wasn't conscious of it, nor of the people around her, she moved to the piano and sat down. There was a sort of stunned silence. Those who made a habit of ignoring others couldn't understand being ignored themselves.

Sherry McKay said, "Someone you know, Bill?"

He roused himself. "Yes."

"Should I be jealous?"

He didn't answer that. Carmelita was playing now, softly. The ceiling lights went out and a diffused spot picked her up and the orchestra came in even more softly, under the piano. She began to sing.

After it was all over she got up and looked at Romero, standing there on the edge of the spot, as though she didn't quit know what to do next. There was a lot of applause this time. It seemed genuine. She turned and stared into the darkness surrounding her. It was almost as though she were looking for someone. "Thank you." Swiftly, then, the curtains enfolded her and she was gone.

Rather feverishly the orchestra went into a dance number.

The lights came on.

Rye saw Izzy Arnstein and Patterson Powers skirting the edge of the room, heading for the curtained arch. They disappeared through it. Rye stood up. "You'll have to get along by yourself for a little while, Sherry." He too skirted the dance floor and entered the passage beyond the curtains. A sextet of chorus girls squealed a little as he looked in on them. He went on until he could hear Powers' voice, and Arnstein's, behind a closed door. Arnstein was talking very fast, Powers hardly at all.

"It's a chance, kid," Arnstein said. "I can use you, but Mr. Powers can really give you a spot where you'll show up to better advantage. He gets the carriage trade that likes things quiet."

"Don't push her," Powers said quietly. "Let her make up her own mind."

"Well, sure, but — " Arnstein had what he thought was an inspiration. "Maybe you'd like to talk to Mr. Rye first, eh?"

Powers did not raise his voice but his surprise was evident. "Would that be William Rye, Callahan's liquor-guzzling bloodhound?"

"Sure, he's the one brought her in."

Carmelita said distinctly, "I never want to see Mr. Rye again."

Izzy Arnstein must have realized then that there was something going on he didn't know about. "Now look, kid, I — "

"That's all right, isn't it?" Powers said. His voice was quietly amused. "If she doesn't want to see Rye again, she doesn't have to, does she?" The door knob rattled. "We'll wait outside till you're ready."

Rye backed into an empty dressing room across the passage. Powers and Arnstein came out. As they went along the hall Arnstein's voice drifted back. "I don't want any trouble, Pat, but — "

"There won't be any trouble," Powers assured him. A blast of music from the supper room drowned the quiet, emotionless voice. The sextet pranced out of their dressing room and through the heavily curtained arch.

Rye crossed the hall and opened Carmelita's door. Then, very quickly, he went in and closed it behind him. "Hello, little one."

She had her dress half over her head, which helped to muffle her first scream. By the time she was ready for the second Rye had a hand on her mouth and was holding her tightly. "Carmelita!"

She fought him stubbornly, her lithe young body like an eel in his arms. "You tricked me. You killed him, you and your damn' Callahan, and now you will kill me too!"

"Be quiet!"

Her small sharp teeth sank into the fleshy part of his palm, and for a moment the pain was so exquisite that he loosed his hold on her. She slipped out of the dress, and his arms, like water down a drain. But she did not scream again. It wasn't necessary. Pat Powers opened the door. Behind him loomed the gorilla known as Joe.

Powers took in the scene, the girl huddled in the corner, one hand over her mouth and her eyes wide with horror; Rye standing there rather foolishly holding her dress. "Well," he said, "I'd no idea you had to use force these days." He jerked his head. "Joe."

Joe came in past him. In the almost palpitant silence the click of the hammer on the gun in his hand was as loud as a snapping whip.

His mouth was contorted in a grimace of pleasurable anticipation. "Give her her dress."

Powers continued to lean in the doorway.

Carmelita's eyes were starey, frightened. Her small breasts rose and fell unevenly. There was a drop of blood, probably Rye's, on her nether lip.

"All right," Rye said. He took a step towards the girl, holding the billowy silk out in his two hands. He threw the dress over Joe's gun and followed it, pinioning Joe's right arm. Joe let go of the gun and buried his left fist to the wrist in Rye's stomach. An agonized sound came out of Rye's mouth. He began to fold. Joe straightened him out with a second blow, this one to the throat. Rye did not know it when he hit the floor.

CHAPTER 11

IZZY ARNSTEIN was bending over him, and in the doorway which so recently had framed Patterson Powers stood Sherry McKay. "I was beginning to think I'd have to pay for my own dinner," she said.

Rye tried to speak and discovered that he couldn't. The blow on his throat had done his vocal chords no good whatever. He sat up and almost passed out again as his stomach muscles cried out and knotted themselves into ropes of sheer agony. He rolled over and lay flat on his belly for a moment. When next he was conscious of Sherry she was on her knees beside him and there was a glass of water in her hand. He propped himself on an elbow and drank a little of it. His voice came back with a rush. "Thanks, pal." After a while he drank a little more water.

Izzy Arnstein began moving nervously about the room. "I'd like to know what goes on, Mr. Rye." His eyes were harried. "Not that I want any part of it, you understand. I've just got to protect myself in the clinches."

Rye refused Sherry's arm and attained his feet all by himself. He stood there, swaying a little from the effort. "Sure, I'm afraid of him too." His eyes were muddy looking. "The best thing you can do, Izzy, is just forget the whole thing. Forget I brought her in, forget you ever saw her." He began to laugh, soundlessly, with the effect of hiccups.

Arnstein said worriedly, "I don't think he's feeling so good, Miss McKay. Maybe — "

She shook her head. "Let him alone, Izzy. He's just been playing God and found out that he isn't omnipotent after all. It's upset him a little."

Rye looked around for his hat. "Let's get out of here." At the door he paused. "Did all that just happen, Izzy, or did you maybe call Powers up?" He watched Arnstein's face get the color of very old linen. "We'd better straighten that out, hadn't we?"

Arnstein licked his lips. "I swear to God it just happened. Powers was short a singer and dropped in to see what he could borrow." He spread his hands. "I was a little afraid of her. I've been afraid of her ever since Holly brought her back this evening." He appealed to Sherry. "You were out front, you saw her." And when she nodded: "The fact is, in some ways she's too good for my place, and in other ways she ain't good enough. Christ, I — "

Rye's lean brown fingers massaged his stomach muscles, hard. "So Powers liked her and you brought him back."

"That's right." Hesitantly, but with a great regard for accuracy, Arnstein repeated the entire conversation Rye had overheard and some that he hadn't. "She said she never wanted to see you again."

"That's what I thought she said."

Arnstein seemed relieved rather than startled at the knowledge that Rye had been listening. "Well, so after we went out, Powers thought maybe his strong-arm boy could give her a lift with her stuff — " He avoided Rye's stare. "I guess you know what happened from then on in."

"Yes," Rye said. He saw that the dressing room was indeed empty of all but the furniture. The curiously muddy look had left his eyes and his smile was almost back to normal when he said, "Powers tell you about it?"

Arnstein grew red in the face, looked embarrassedly at Sherry.

She said, "Don't mind me, Izzy. Was there a struggle?"

"Something about her dress being ripped off," Arnstein admitted. He shrugged his thin shoulders. "Of course, I been around too long to believe all I hear, but — " Quite suddenly he became indignant. "God damn it, Rye, she went out of here under her own power. Nobody was pushing her!"

"Forget it," Rye said.

Arnstein was still angry. "That's what Powers suggested too." His mouth writhed with self pity. "Sure, just forget it, Izzy. Don't give it another thought, Izzy. Just let a lot of gangsters and thugs come in and ruin your digestion for weeks, and then laugh it off like it was vitamins!"

"I'm sorry," Rye said with the utmost sincerity. He really was. He thought of what Sherry had said about his playing at being God. Maybe that was it — he had angered some other and greater deity. There was no other way he could account for Gerald's causing Blossom Dee's absence, and Blossom's absence making it necessary for Pat Powers to get a substitute canary, and thinking of the greatest clearing house of all, Arnstein's, and picking the one girl out of all the world who was the most apt to pull Gerald's father down into the nethermost pit of political oblivion. It was all so beautifully logical, so mathematically perfect that Rye wondered at his own temerity in thinking he could outwit it. He said, "Well, thanks for this and that, Izzy. I'll try to make it up to you sometime." He looked at Sherry. "Coming?"

The color in her cheeks deepened a trifle. "Now that you mention it, yes." She did not take his arm. "Good-night, Izzy."

They went out and down the passage, out into the great noisy supper room, through that to the checkroom, got their things and presently found his car in the parking lot. He helped her in. "I'll take you home, Sherry."

She shook her head. "No."

"What do you mean, no?" He went around and opened the other door and got in beside her. "I've some things to do."

She stared straight through the windshield. In the reflected light from the dash her profile was as clearcut as a cameo. "Still playing God?"

He remained perfectly quiet for a moment. "That's the second time you've said that tonight. The first time we weren't alone."

"You were alone when they almost killed you," she reminded him. There was a sound as though she might be laughing. She wasn't. "Always alone. Always the great William Rye, the Mr. Fixit for Calexico Oil, the strong silent man who keeps Callahan's muddy boots clean for him, the — " She was frankly crying now, though not noisily. "What am I supposed to do, be an iron woman?"

Rye leaned forward and switched on the motor and nosed the Buick into Wilshire traffic. The wind was stronger now, and there were only occasional patches of fog. A thousand multi-colored signs heralded the Miracle Mile. "I had no idea you felt that way about Callahan."

"What way?"

"You sound as though you almost hated him."

She got a handkerchief out of her bag and dabbed at her eyes. "I don't hate him, except for what he's done to you."

"He hasn't done anything to me."

"Hasn't he?" Her voice was under perfect control again, a little tired, a little cynical, but at least she was through crying. "I've been his private secretary for almost as long as you've been his Number One boy."

Rye's face became wooden. "So you saw that too." He halted the car for a red light. It wasn't till after the light had changed to green and he had driven another three blocks that he said, quite gently for him, "Callahan saved my life once, Sherry. He took a chance to do it, a chance of losing a lot of things he prized rather highly." The headlights of oncoming cars outlined the hard jut of his jaw. His eyes were in shadow. "No matter whether you admire his brilliance or marvel at his occasional stupidities you don't forget a thing like that."

She drew a deep breath. "No, I suppose you don't."

"Then you're not angry with me any more?"

She moved a little away from him at that. Gloved fingers drew the collar of her fur coat tighter about her throat. "Do you think I'd care what happened to you if I didn't — if we weren't — " She looked out at the passing lights. "All right, don't tell me anything you don't want to. And please take me home now."

In the apartment he took her in his arms and pressed his mouth to hers. "You're rather a nice person, Sherry. Remind me to mention it again some time, will you?" He went to the telephone and called his own apartment and asked for messages.

The clerk said Mrs. Callahan had been trying to get him. "It seemed pretty urgent, Mr. Rye."

Rye frowned. "You're sure it wasn't Mr. Callahan?" The clerk was quite sure. "All right," Rye said, "I'll call her back." He gave the number of the Bel Air house.

It was Van Sweringen who finally answered. "Mr. Rye," he said, very low, "do you think you could come out here for a little while? Mrs. Callahan is terribly upset."

"About what?" Rye demanded sharply.

Van Sweringen's surprise was obvious. "Why, hadn't you heard, sir? Mr. Callahan has been arrested."

CHAPTER 12

"WELL, Sybil?" Rye said. He stood just inside the door of her private sitting room, watching her. In a way the room was a great deal like Sybil herself, perfect down to the last minute detail. Whites and off-whites predominated, virginal, a trifle cold. In a diaphanous pale gold negligee Sybil was having a mild fit of hysterics on the chaise longue before a fire whose flames seemed to have been measured and gauged by the interior decorator. On a low table beside her there was a crystal decanter of Scotch, also pale gold, to match the negligee and her hair.

"Bill, you've got to *do* something!"

He came and sat beside her on the couch. "All right. What would you suggest?"

"You're so cold," she complained. With a bit of pale gold chiffon she stifled a sob. "Gerald's gone, and now Ed, and oh, Bill, I'm *frightened!*" She smelled pleasantly of Scotch and Chanel No. 5.

He put an arm around her. He felt that to be perfectly in keeping with his surroundings he should drape a handkerchief over his lapel, like an antimacassar. "That better?"

Sighing, she relaxed against his shoulder. "Hold me tighter." Her body presently ceased its trembling. The tears had left her cheeks unmarred. After a time she said in a muffled voice, "What will they do to him, Bill?"

"Work on him for a little while. Talk to him. Try to find a motive."

Her blue eyes opened very wide. "But the gun? His fingerprints?"

"Bad," Rye agreed. "Very bad." The fingerprints were going to be the worst. The gun, even though it was Callahan's, could be explained as a frame, but the fingerprints in Lou Small's hallway were going to be harder, indeed almost impossible. You didn't frame fingerprints except in elaborately illogical B pictures. "The police have got enough to hold him on. They can't convict him without proving a motive."

He got in his car and drove back to town by way of Sunset and Beverly Boulevard. City Hall was lit up like a Christmas tree. So too was the County Building, opposite. Though the news had not yet broken on the streets, those that were in the know, politicians and cops and newspapermen, were thick enough in the corridors to impede Rye's progress toward the Detective Bureau. A couple of reporters on the police beat hailed him. He let them haul him into the press room, where there were some more reporters.

"Statement, Mr. Rye?"

He grinned at them, even the *Post-Express* man. "Did Callahan give you a statement?"

"Sure, he said it was a frame."

"Then I'll give you one too," Rye said. "It's a frame."

"Then how do you explain the gun and the fingerprints? Who do you suggest is framing him?"

Rye looked at the *Post-Express* man. "If I suggested anything like that it would be actionable, wouldn't it?" He watched the man's face turn beet red. "Same like if your sheet allowed anything but the facts to creep in."

"Now look, Rye, I'm just a guy working for a living."

"Sure," Rye said. He singled out the man from the *Chronicle*. "Tell Murphy I'll drop up later with some evidence." Murphy was the city editor of the friendly morning paper. The other morning papers would hold off until they saw what the *Chronicle* would do. The *Post-Express*, on the other hand, calling itself "The twenty-four hour newspaper," had an edition coming out anywhere from six to twelve times a day. The trucks were probably already rolling with the latest, and whatever Granger had chosen to say, he couldn't very well kill it now. Rye hoped they had been sure enough of themselves to get careless and leave out some of the usual alleged's and its various synonyms. He was still pretty angry with Mr. Weldon Granger and the *Post-Express* for the editorial squib which had precipitated Carmelita into the arms of Pat Powers. "Where are they holding Callahan?"

"In the Bureau."

"Thanks." Rye went on down the long corridor and around an ell to Inspector Cain's office. It could have been the office of a railway magnate. The police department had outgrown the golden-oak-and-cuspidor stage. At one of the two big desks in the carpeted anteroom a well-dressed woman of forty was typing industriously. At the other desk sat Lieutenant Belarski. He did not belong there. The man who did belong there was probably closeted with Cain himself, behind the closed door of the inner office.

Belarski got slowly to his feet. "I've been expecting you," he said. There were pouches under his eyes and the whites were a little bloodshot.

Rye looked at the closed door. "Cain in?"

"You don't need Cain," Belarski said. "I'll show you where Callahan is. Friedlander is with him." His smile was thin and without warmth. "Surprised?"

Rye shook his head. "I hardly expected you to be working him over with a sap." He looked at the typist who was carefully minding her own business. "Not yet, and not here."

"Of course," Belarski said, "I don't have to let you see him if I don't want to," He cracked the knuckles in one of his bony hands. "His attorney, yes, but not you."

"I know," Rye said amiably. "You don't have to but you will, and in return for the favor you'd like to have a little talk with me afterward. You'd like to ask me what the hell Callahan's motive is." He looked at the woman. "Will you excuse the naughty word?"

She pretended not to hear him. The inner door opened and Inspector Cain and Floyd Ingram, the District Attorney, appeared very surprised to see Rye standing there. "Well, Mr. Rye," Cain said pleasantly. He was a tall, stoop-shouldered man of fifty or so, with the quiet, assured manner of the pastor of one of the wealthier churches.

'Hello," Rye said, just as pleasantly. He rather liked the chief of detectives. He looked at the paunchy, pompous, but somewhat younger edition of Weldon Granger who was Floyd Ingram, "Evening, Prosecutor."

"Ah, good evening, Mr. Rye." Ingram tossed his mane like a spirited horse. "I'd like you to understand that there is nothing personal in this — ah — unfortunate business." He was referring to the fact that the Callahan machine had opposed him in the last election. He could afford to be magnanimous, because he had won. "This case will be tried strictly on its merits."

"It hasn't any merits," Rye said.

The district attorney flushed angrily. "Are you insinuating, sir, that — "

Rye denied that he was insinuating anything. "I just don't think the case has any merit — as a case." He appealed to Inspector Cain. "I can think that if I want to, can't I?"

"Naturally we can't stop you from thinking," Cain admitted. He looked at his watch. "Belarski, see that Mr. Rye gets in to Callahan any time he wants to."

"Well, thanks," Rye said. He had the uncomfortable feeling that they were all holding something back. Except for Ingram's one little flare-up it was all too polite, too genteel. "What gave you the idea it was Callahan in the first place? I thought you were working on some 'Mystery Woman' angle."

Cain shook his head regretfully. "That washed out."

Rye's spirits lifted a trifle. It was nice to know that at least one of your stratagems had worked. He said, "I don't like to go on record as a prophet, but I'll give you odds this'll wash out too." His eyes were bright and intent on the district attorney's face. "These anonymous tips always backfire."

Belarski lost his temper. "I'll take that bet." His thin lips writhed. "I've been waiting a long time for this chance to get you, and by God I'll — "

"Lieutenant!" Cain said sharply.

Rye continued to look at Ingram. "Bail?"

"Over my dead body, sir!"

"All right," Belarksi said. He didn't even offer to frisk Rye for a gun. He waved at the solid-paneled inner door. "You can go in whenever you feel like it." He turned on his heel and went out. Rye opened the inner door.

Except for the bars on the windows high up in the far wall there was no suggestion of a cell about the room. There was a leather couch and a big table and some chairs. Callahan and Harris Friedlander were seated at the table, between them a box of Callahan's cigars and a bottle and some glasses and a pitcher of ice water. "Well," Rye said, "all the comforts of home!" He came in and closed the door and leaned against it.

Callahan looked pretty good, considering. His iron gray hair was neatly brushed, his mustache crisp and bristly over a mouth that was a little too taut but not discouraged. His eyes were angry rather than worried. "It's about time you got here."

Friedlander was his lean dark handsome self. The white carnation in his lapel looked as though it had just come from a florist's icebox. "Hello, Rye."

Rye acknowledged the salutation, but his eyes were still busy with the room. Finally he went over and got down on his knees and looked under the couch. After a while he found the microphone. "Calling all cars," he said loudly. "Calling all cars." He pulled some of the wire up through the tiny hole in the floor, put a kink in it and with a quick jerk snapped it like a piece of string. He got up, brushing his knees a little absently. "I hope you guys haven't been discussing secrets."

One of the cops opened the door, looked angrily at Rye, said, "Excuse me, I thought I heard something drop."

"A pin," Rye said. "These modern devices are wonderful. They pick up the slightest sound. Hope you don't mind, officer."

The cop banged the door shut. Friedlander said worriedly, "Now see here, Rye, there's no use antagonizing these fellows. Besides, we haven't anything to conceal." His sharp eyes probed Rye's face. "Or have we?"

"I don't know," Rye said. "I'm just as confused as the police." He looked at Callahan. "You knock him off, Ed?"

"You know damned well I — " Callahan's strong white teeth tore the end off a fresh cigar. "No!"

Rye smiled at Friedlander. "All right, then it's simple, isn't it? All you've got to do is tell the papers that it's so ridiculous, so obviously a frame, that you're not even going to hire a criminal attorney."

"But — " Friedlander glared at him. "How did you know I was going to hire a criminal lawyer?"

"Because it's the first thing a corporation lawyer would think of." Rye shook his head. "It's also an admission that there's something to defend." He was polite, but insistent. "You see that, don't you?"

Friedlander was not dumb. "Putting it that way, I suppose you're right. Just the same, I'd like to get Callahan out of here."

"Let him stay in a while," Rye said. "It'll keep him out of trouble. Besides, the longer he's in, the more he'll have to yell about when we do spring him."

Callahan bridled. "Don't mind me, you bastards. Just go ahead and talk as though I still wore diapers." The tiny veins in his nose and cheeks were an angry red. "Christ!"

Friedlander thrust his cigar back and got up. "Well — "

"Sure," Rye said, "go right ahead, Fried. I've got one or two things to talk over with him about another matter, but after that I'll get busy on this." He looked at Callahan. "You deny being in that office building?"

"Yes."

Rye frowned. "That was bad. You knew they found your fingerprints, didn't you?"

"Not when they asked me." Callahan's voice was bitter. "I haven't had as much experience with these things as some people I could spit on."

Rye was reminded of Sherry McKay's indictment. She had not

mentioned Callahan spitting on him. He put the thought from him. "Well, we'll just have to refresh your memory, that's all. You can be thinking about it all night, and finally you'll remember that you did go to see somebody in that building." He held up a hand. "No, not *last* night. A long time ago."

Friedlander cursed. "I won't be a party to anything like that, Rye. Suborning witnesses, perjury — "

Rye stared at him in apparent surprise. "Did I ask you to? I merely said that Callahan must have had a lapse of memory." His eyes grew dark and humid looking. "Is there any other way that you can explain his fingerprints on that wall?"

Friedlander flushed. "I won't be — " He bit his laps. "Well — "

"That's fine," Rye said. After a while he said, "If it comes to that — suborning and perjury and so on — we'll have a criminal lawyer who thinks more of getting his client off than he does of the Bar Association." He held out his hand. "No offense, Fried?"

"No," Friedlander said. He shook the hand, said a rather shamefaced goodnight to Callahan, picked up his hat and stick and departed. In the anteroom Lieutenant Belarski was arguing with the two cops. Rye closed the door and went over and sat opposite Callahan. "Well, Ed?" He tried not to look at Callahan's hands. It was pretty difficult. He kept seeing a woman's throat above a white tatting collar whose pattern was as distinct as though it were right there in front of him. He thought it was funny that this should bother him more than Lou Small. Well, not funny, exactly. He lit a cigar with fingers that shook a little. No, certainly not funny. "I told you this was dynamite, Ed. Remember?"

Callahan got up and began pacing the room, a square, thick-set man whom a great many people had no reason to love. "The first decent impulse I've had in years and I land in the can for it." He felt of his throat as though expecting to find the noose already there. "All I wanted was to see she was taken care of and — "

Rye was surprised to discover that he had unconsciously blown a smoke ring. "That isn't quite true, Ed. You wanted her, too, and I told you you couldn't have her, remember?"

Callahan flung his cigar savagely into a corner of the room. "I wish to Christ you'd quit saying 'I told you so!' "

"All right. But if you'd only learn to let me — "

One of the cops opened the door. "Everything under control in here?"

Rye looked at him. "Would you mind bringing me a fresh hacksaw blade? I just broke my last one."

The door banged shut.

Callahan resumed his nervous pacing. "I suppose she'd like nothing better than to see 'em throw the book at me." He regarded Rye from beneath half-lowered lids. "Where is she?"

"You're a hard man to convince," Rye sighed. He decided he wouldn't tell Callahan where Carmelita was — or how she had got there. "Let's talk about the gun instead. That gun rather ruins some of my pet theories about Small's unfortunate end." He examined the tip of his cigar. "And believe me, I do mean unfortunate, Ed."

Callahan gnawed at his nether lip. "You're telling me." After a while, avoiding Rye's intent gaze, he said, "If I remember right, one of your pet theories was that I did it."

Rye nodded.

Callahan looked at him. "You still think I did?"

"We needn't go into that just now," Rye said. "Whether you did or didn't, I still have to get you out of here."

"I'll be God damned if you do!"

The tiny muscle at the corner of Rye's mouth began to twitch. Let's talk about the gun," he suggested quietly. "Where did you keep it, when did you see it last, had it been cleaned and who could have got it?"

"How do I know?" Callahan demanded, tackling the questions in reverse order." Any one of the servants, half a dozen callers beside the governor, Quarrie himself, the state troopers — "

Ignoring the sarcasm Rye carefully wrote down the names of the callers. None of them seemed to fit as a possible conspirator in a plot to ruin Callahan, but any of them certainly could have gotten the gun. Callahan had kept it in his desk in the library, and the library windows opened on a terrace, thus making it not too unlikely that a prowler might have entered from outside. Callahan swore he hadn't seen the thing in a month of Sundays. The police swore that he had, and that he had cleaned it very thoroughly indeed after using it on a shabby little private dick named Lou Small.

"All right," Rye said. He was sorry he couldn't introduce the subject of Mrs. Kampf. Neither the cops nor the newspapers appeared to know about that yet, and it would be better if his own knowledge remained a secret for a little while. He could see no reason for Callahan to have done for her too, but then he could see no reason for anybody else either — with the possible exception of El Segundo Ruiz. He decided that he really must do something about Ruiz, and about Carmelita. With the headlines announcing Callahan's arrest would come a break of some kind; especially if it became known that the police were in the dark as to a motive. Carmelita could furnish it. So could Ruiz, but of the two, Carmelita was the most likely to act first. It was she who had wanted nothing but revenge. Ruiz, on the other hand, would try to figure a profit for himself, to offset the one he had expected to get. If he were very clever, and had friends in town who could tip him off to the political situation, he might even try to peddle his information to Mr. Weldon Granger. Or peddle his silence to Callahan, through William Rye. Rye rather looked forward to a visit from El Segundo tonight; tomorrow at the latest. He stood up. "Keep an eye on the papers, Ed. There's a chiropractor in that building that maybe I can work on, but you'd better not remember your visit to him till I see you again."

"A chiropractor!" Callahan sneered. "What the hell would I be doing with a muscle kneader?"

"Maybe you fell down," Rye said. "Maybe a charley horse ran up and bit you."

Callahan followed him to the door. "Quarrie will see the papers and want to do something. Tell him to sit tight, will you?"

"Sure, I'll tell him." Rye opened the door and went out, smiling pleasantly at the two cops. They did not return his smile. You could see they hated his guts for finding the microphone. One of them said, "There's nothing I hate worse'n a smart guy," and the other said, "Yeah, me too," and spat.

Belarski was nowhere in sight. He was nowhere in sight until Rye was out in the dark little side street where he had left his car and actually had one foot on the running board. Then Belarski was there, and Belarski's partner and another man almost as big. "Now we'll have that little talk you spoke about," Belarski said.

Rye took his foot off the running board. "Can't we make it some other time, Nick? I'm in something of a hurry."

"Now," Belarski said. He and the other men crowded Rye against the side of the car.

"All right, if you're going to be tough about it." Rye's first traveled perhaps six inches and hit Belarski in the mouth. Belarski fell down. Rye ducked under the full-armed blow aimed at him by Belarski's partner, but the third man tripped him and he too fell down. Presently it became evident that three men, two of them with saps, were better than one man with nothing but fists.

CHAPTER 13

HE opened his eyes on a room so typical of the third rate hotel, the dollar-a-night-and-no-questions-asked kind, that he knew immediately why he was there. It and others just like it had taken the place of the outmoded goldfish room at Headquarters. The purpose was the same.

There was an iron bed, a dresser with a chipped mirror, a washbasin with open plumbing in the corner and a couple of rickety chairs, A not-too-clean woolen blanket was fastened over the one window with thumb tacks. Water gurgled in the trap of the washbasin, and Lieutenant Belarski had a soggy, rope-like towel in his hands. Hefty, Belarski's overgrown partner, was examining a raw red welt on his thick wrist, where the thong of his sap had cut into it. The third man was not in evidence. A sickly ceiling light turned Rye's face butter yellow, though except for a certain puffiness about the mouth and eyes he did not look as bad as he felt. The rickety chair creaked under his weight as he twisted his head back and forth. The muscles in his neck and shoulders creaked too.

Belarski threw the wet towel at him. "Wipe the blood off your mouth."

"Why? So you can start all over again?"

"You're taking the wrong attitude," Belarski said. He affected the patient air of a parent explaining something to a recalcitrant child. "All you've got to do is tell us one thing. Just one little thing, that's all."

Rye used the towel gingerly. "All right."

"Why'd he do it?"

Rye shook his head. "I don't know."

Belarski looked at Hefty. "I'm afraid he's going to be stubborn."

"Yeah."

Rye attempted to get out of the chair, but his legs were rubber. He flicked the towel at Hefty's eyes. He was no good at that, either. Hefty caught the loose end in his left hand and perked it free. With his right hand he brought the sap down hard across the bridge of Rye's nose. The room went round and round for an instant, and freshets of water came out of Rye's eyes and ran down and were salty on his lips. Distantly, wavily, Belarski's voice reached his consciousness. "Why'd he do it? Why'd he do it?"

"I don't know."

This went on for some time. Occasionally the big man with the sap would vary the target. In his way, Hefty was an artist. Occasionally the room and all in it would black out, and once Rye found that the rickety chair had finally collapsed under him, but the inexorable voice continued. "Why'd he do it, Rye? We know he did it. All we've got to know is why? After that we'll take you home."

Rye could not see them very well any more. All he knew was that every time he said, "I don't know," the sap would try to beat his brains out. And if he didn't say it, if cunningly he kept his mouth shut and said nothing at all, they would think he had passed out and revive him with methods even more painful than the persuader. It was during one of these latter periods that Sherry McKay opened the door. "That will be enough of that," she said quietly. At least it seemed to Rye that she said it quietly. He was not quite all there. He did not believe that Sherry was there either. She was just something his imagination had conjured up out of the mists, a vision, and he knew that visions always spoke quietly. His fogged mind struggled with the pistol in her hand. He had never seen a vision with a pistol before. Presently, by a supreme effort, he opened his eyes very wide. "Hello, Vision." It seemed to him that when he said "Vision" it had the sound of a power saw ripping a board.

"Hello, Bill."

He knew then that she was real, but there was nothing that he could do about it. There was nothing that he could do about anything. Invisible shackles held him to the floor amid the ruins of the shattered chair, only his mind coming alive, a spirit detached from the flesh, so that he was able to view the proceedings and his own body lying there as through the eyes of a departed soul. He thought this was a good joke on Hefty and Belarski. They could maul and beat and kick the body of William Rye until they were black in the face, and it wouldn't hurt him at all, because he was no longer in it. He began to laugh, very quietly, because they mustn't learn his secret.

Sherry's voice shook him out of that phase. "Bill, stop it!"

Surprised, he looked at her. "All right, hon." His mouth had the looseness of an idiot's. After a while he got around to looking for Belarski and Hefty. He saw that they were standing flat against the far wall, facing it, arms stretched high up as though trying to reach the jointure between wall and ceiling. It was obvious that the gun in Sherry's hand must be the cause of all this. Rye was vaguely annoyed that he had missed some of the intervening steps. He had not been conscious of her telling them what to do. Maybe they had just known without being told. He recalled that he himself had always been afraid of a gun in a hysterical woman's hand. He wondered if Sherry were hysterical. She didn't look it. "Now kick them away from you," she was saying.

Hefty's foot pawed at a couple of guns lying on the floor. One of them skidded close enough to Rye's hand so that he could pick it up without too much effort. He did that, and the feel of metal rationalized the whole business; it was as though the gun had some inherent strength of its own and was able to impart it to the man. Slowly, very carefully, he got to his hands and knees, and then, using the back of the broken chair for a prop, he attained his feet and stood there, swaying slightly but with everything in focus and crystal sharp. He saw that Sherry had reached the breaking point. "All right, Sherry, it's all right now."

Belarski risked a glance over his shoulder. There was sweat on his face. "You're just making it that much tougher on yourselves."

"Probably," Rye agreed. From the tail of his eye he watched Sherry back to the wall and lean against it. A little color had come back to her cheeks and her eyes were no longer glassy. "What happened to the other guy?"

She shivered. "He's — I put him in the toilet at the end of the hall."

Something about that struck Rye as very funny. "In the toilet." He massaged the back of his neck. "Don't you think that's cute, Nick?"

Belarski didn't think it was cute.

"Well, I think it's cute," Rye said. He lifted the gun. "Get the big fellow's cuffs out and pretend you're great pals, will you?" He shook his head as Belarski offered him an argument. "No, I'm not kidding, Nick. It may be a little embarrassing to be found that way, but not half as embarrassing as — " He addressed Hefty's back. "How do you feel about it, Slewfoot? Would you rather be laughed at or cried over?"

After a while he and Belarski were snugly linked to the foot of the iron bed. Rye went out, leaning heavily on Sherry's shoulder. Together, without hurry, they traversed the long dimlit hall and descended a back stairs to the alley. Rye's car was in the alley. He stumbled a little, getting in, and sudden nausea attacked him and he leaned there in the darkness and was sick.

Sherry's voice came to him. "Oh, my dear, what have they done to you?"

He wiped his mouth on a soggy sleeve. "According to their lights, they're trying to break a murder case." This time, with Sherry's help, he was able to make it into the car, though he did not offer to drive. As they left the alley they heard sounds from up above which indicated Belarski and his partner were becoming restless. The night wind was cool on Rye's face and presently it occurred to him that Sherry's timely appearance was nothing short of a miracle. He asked her about it.

Her voice was not as composed as she would have liked it to be. "I rather expected you to call on Callahan, and I told you before that I was tired of sitting on the sidelines." She trod down harder on the throttle. "This last little episode ought to convince even you that you aren't the Lone Ranger."

"Oh, it does," Rye assured her. His reflection in the side window was oddly distorted and lumpy. He wondered if his nose was broken. He felt of it with tenderly exploring fingers. "So you came down to the Hall and hung around?"

She nodded. She was still angry with him. "I saw those men, Belarski and the others, waiting near your car, but by the time I got to you — to where you'd been — they'd already loaded you into a police car and were leaving." She drew an uneven breath. "It took me a little while to find your spare keys, and after that I had to search the vicinity for the car they'd taken you away in."

"And you found it," Rye said admiringly. He watched Midnight traffic flowing past them. "Tell me about the third man, the one you put in the — er — toilet."

It appeared that Sherry had discovered the detective guarding a certain door, and had thought about screaming for help. "Only screaming might have interfered with the secrecy you're so darned fond of, so I went back and found a brick."

Rye regarded her. "Kill him?"

"No." Her mouth made a firm straight line. "He won't be able to eat for a while."

"Cute," Rye said.

She turned and looked at him. "Isn't it about time that — "

"Yes," Rye said, "it's about time. I'm going to bed and let you get a chiropractor for me."

CHAPTER 14

HE was a raw-boned man of indeterminate age, with dun-colored hair and a seamed face from which the eyes looked out at you with a certain expectancy but not much hope. There was a noticeable shine to his blue serge suit. "Well, young man, what have you been doing to yourself?"

"I've been taking a hot bath and lying here in bed and rubbing ice on my face," Rye said. He rubbed some more ice on it. "And drinking Scotch."

"I didn't mean that." The doctor looked at Sherry, questioning his latest patient's sanity. She paused in the act of removing her coat and performed the introductions. She had no more idea why Rye had wanted this particular chiropractor than the man in the moon. "Mr. Rye — Dr. Knebel."

Dr. Knebel tentatively opened the worn leather bag he was carrying. "If your purpose is to reduce the swelling I'd suggest alternating hot towels with the ice. Perhaps some witch-hazel with the towels." It was clear that he was impressed with the apartment, and with Sheridan McKay, who at Rye's behest had sought him out. About Rye himself the doctor had not yet made up his mind. That put him on a par with Rye. "I suppose you ran into a door?"

"No," Rye said, "I ran into some cops." From beneath lowered lids he watched the seamed face above him. So far as he could tell the doctor neither feared cops nor favored them.

"Hmmm, cops, eh?" Knebel accepted a steaming Turkish towel from Sherry and smothered Rye's face with it. Rye cursed. The doctor thoughtfully made an opening for Rye's nose. He put both large hands on the towel and leaned his weight on it. "This may hurt a little."

Rye's body, under the covers, said that it hurt more than a little. He decided that the cure, if any, was worse than the disease. He wished Sherry would go home, though he knew the wish was not likely to be fulfilled. It occurred to him that maybe she did know why he'd asked for this particular bone-crusher. She'd had to go to Small's office building first, to get the guy's name off the directory. He expelled steam through his nose and wiggled his feet.

The doctor took the towel off and substituted another, this one thin and saturated with witch-hazel and something faintly reminicent of racing stables. In the brief interim between the two there was time for no more than a quick glance at Sherry's face. She looked tired. Beautiful as ever, but tired. Curiously, seen from this angle, her eyes looked green. Another hot towel plopped down, driving the liniment home. Rye was positive that when this one was removed the flesh would come with it. He forced his mind from this gruesome thought by concentrating on a couple of ribs that were giving him hell.

Rye rubbed ice on his nose. Now that some of the puffiness was gone from around his eyes he didn't look so bad. "You're smart, Doc," he said admiringly. He saw that Sherry, standing there at the foot of the bed, was regarding him with a rather strained expression. "Show him the latest edition of the *Post-Express*, Sherry."

She got it from the dresser. This time the banner read: GOVERNOR'S FRIEND AND BACKER ARRESTED FOR MURDER! Beneath that a double column went on to relate the facts against Callahan; the gun and the fingerprints and his lack of an alibi. Granger's hirelings had been very careful to steer clear of motivation, but without actually saying so they managed to convey that murder was just one of the lesser evils of machine politics. There was nothing that the *Post-Express* could be sued for, not even the bracketed photographs of Quarrie and Callahan, though the obvious inference was that if Callahan had committed murder the governor must have known about it. District Attorney Floyd Ingram came in for a nice plug. He would prosecute the case without fear and without favor. He was the champion of "The Little People, Crying in the Wilderness."

Knebel's large bony hands folded the paper carefully. His seamed face was expressionless. "I take it that you want something beside my professional services."

Rye put the remains of the piece of ice in his mouth. "Did I say so?" He was careful to avoid the look in Sherry's eyes. They were riveted on his face with a kind of shocked disbelief. "Of course, if you were willing to take my word for it that he didn't do it — that it's just the old political badger racket at work — " He winced as Knebel taped the area around his ribs. "It's a shame a man of your calibre should be buried in a place like the Weiler Building."

Knebel compressed his lips, but said nothing.

"I've perjured myself lots of times," Rye said.

One of Knebel's fingers prodded some black and blue spots he had missed before. "I see you have."

Sherry cried out at that. "This is unspeakable!"

"But necessary," Rye said. His eyes were bright and hard. "Fire with fire, you know, that sort of thing." He looked at the chiropractor. "I'll bet you could do a lot of things with, say ten grand, Doc. I'll bet you could even let the police work you over a little bit, though I don't think that will happen."

Knebel licked his lips. "Your word of honor that Callahan isn't guilty?"

"Word of honor."

Sherry's face was white. "Honor!" She tried one last appeal on Knebel. "Believe me, he doesn't know the meaning of the word. He'd sacrifice you in a minute if it were necessary to save — "

"He hasn't sacrificed Callahan to save himself some rather painful injuries," Knebel pointed out. He wiped his mouth on the back of a hand. "I think I'll take a chance on you, son. It was — er — an even ten thousand you said?"

Rye looked at Sherry. "In my pants you'll find a couple of thousand or so. Get that and some paper, will you?"

"I won't!" She turned and went swiftly into the living room. After a while the hall door opened and closed. For a time there was no sound at all in the apartment. It was as though both men were waiting for her to come back. She did not.

CHAPTER 15

OVER a breakfast tray on which were two two-minute eggs, some crisp bacon and toast and a pot of coffee, Rye considered the *Morning Chronicle,* also brought him by the elevator boy. A ten o'clock morning sun poured in the wide-open windows and laid a path across the rose-taupe carpet through the connecting door and all the way to the hall door on the far side of the living room. Though he was still in bed, this was pure luxury. Dr. Knebel had done a pretty good job, and on the whole Rye looked and felt almost normal. Beneath the covers a gun was warm and comforting against his thigh. The hall door was unlocked.

Murphy, of the *Chronicle,* had made as fair a case for Callahan as he could without leaving himself out on a limb. He had only tentatively accepted Rye's word about a surprise witness, and his front page was larded with such loopholes as "It is alleged" and "Authoritative sources report." The general tenor, however, was all that Rye could have expected and would serve to partially mitigate the attack by the *Post-Express.* You were led to believe that with Callahan's fingerprints logically yet innocently accounted for, and with no motive proven or even hinted at, there was nothing left but the gun, a palpable frame-up if the *Chronicle* had ever seen one. The *Chronicle* called attention to similar "jobs" within its memory, and asked pointedly if anyone seriously believed that a man smart enough to head a vast enterprise like Calexico Oil and control an "alleged political machine" would be so naive as to retain possession of the weapon with which he had committed a murder. "Don't make us laugh!" the *Chronicle* enjoined its readers.

Rye cautiously bit into a piece of toast. His jaws were still sore and his teeth had scored the inside of his lips, but the teeth themselves were secure and all accounted for. He found that by first coating his mouth with egg and then dunking the toast in coffee he could eat with practically no irritation. At his elbow the telephone rang. "Yes?"

It was the State Capital calling, and presently Governor Quarrie himself came on the wire. His voice was smooth and unruffled. If he were worried he hid it. "Is there any chance of their making this stick?"

"There's always a chance," Rye said. "You see the papers yet?"

"Only the *Post-Express.*"

"Get the *Chronicle,*" Rye advised him. "Unless the police or the district attorney can adduce more evidence; unless they can put the screws on every magistrate in town, we can spring Callahan on bail any time we want to."

Quarrie's voice sharpened a trifle. "I can influence a few magistrates myself!"

"But you won't," Rye said. "That's exactly what Granger is hoping you'll do." He cradled the phone in the angle between his neck and shoulder and used his hands to find and light a cigarette. "Callahan suggested that you don't even make a statement. The whole thing is beneath your dignity, get it? It's too ridiculous."

There was a brief hiatus. Then Quarrie said, very low, "All right, tell Ed not to worry." He drew an audible breath. "If necessary there's always executive clemency."

Someone knocked on the hall door. Rye pushed the tray aside and lay back against the pillows. His right hand was not in sight. His eyes watched the path of sunlight his visitors must traverse. "Come in!"

Patterson Powers was in a hard-twisted salt-and-pepper gray. In the sunlight there was a chrome-plate sheen to it, a reflection of the quality in his eyes. Behind him lounged the hulk known as Joe, recognizable instantly because of the toothpick which seemed as much a part of him as the tongue which worried it. Without hurry they negotiated the distance between hall and bedroom doors. Powers was angry and trying not to show it. Joe apparently had no feeling one way or the other. His eyes were the color of wet sand.

Rye waved a hand, the left one. "Chair?"

Powers declined with a brief shake of the head. He had not removed his hat. "This won't take very long, Rye." For the first time he appeared to notice that Rye was in bed. "Been having trouble?"

"Cops," Rye said.

"Cops are bad," Powers agreed quietly. His not-unhealthy pallor gave his square strong face the quality of granite. "You're sure your trouble wasn't with a girl?"

Rye looked at Joe. He wondered where it would hurt Joe most to be shot. "I'm sorry, I haven't had time to do very much about Blossom, Pat. I've been busy."

Joe's mouth and toothpick contrived a particularly unpleasant sneer. "Maybe you've been too busy."

"I wasn't thinking of Blossom," Powers said. "Not for the moment, anyway. I meant the young lady who said she never wanted to see you again." The cloth of his coat made little ripples of halation in the sunlight. "I had an idea you hadn't respected her wishes."

Beneath the covers, Rye's muscles tightened. His face was expressionless, wooden. "Whatever gave you that impression?"

"She's gone," Powers said. "She did one show for me and then vanished. I don't think she took a powder all by herself."

"You're suggesting that I kidnapped her?"

"I'm suggesting that the last time I saw you, you seemed to want her pretty bad."

Joe wagged his head. "Yeah, pretty bad." His consideration of Rye was mildly resentful. "You mean them cops could put you in bed when I couldn't?"

"Don't take it to heart," Rye said. "There were three of them." He looked at Powers. "It seems to me you're having rather a tough time keeping track of your girls lately, Pat. First Blossom, now this one." He made his voice deliberately insulting. "If you ask me, I don't think either one of them has vanished, at least not without your help. Certainly not with mine."

Joe made a guttural sound deep in his throat and took a step toward the bed. Powers lifted a hand. "Joe!"

Rye said, "Your boss is smarter than you are, Joe. He knows I'm not going to let you get close to me a second time." The gun in his hand made a suggestive bulk under the blankets. "This time I'm in my own corral."

Powers said, "Joe," again, more softly, and Joe returned to his former position. His toothpick snapped. He started to reach for another one, thought better of it. Something stirred far back in the opaque, wet-sand eyes, but he said nothing.

"I'll tell you something else," Rye said angrily. "I'm getting sick and tired of having you move in on me whenever you feel like it. I don't know where Blossom is and I don't care." He stared very hard at the granite pallor of Powers' face. "Want me to hazard a guess as to what really happened in her case?"

"It might be interesting," Powers said.

The palm of Rye's hand was sweaty where he held the gun, but in his way he was as good a gambler as the man who made a business of gambling. "I don't blame you for being sore. Maybe I'd have been sore myself. Maybe I'd have been sore enough to have her knocked off and then pretend she'd run away."

"You son of a bitch," Joe said. He looked appealingly at Powers. "Boss, can I — ?"

"No," Powers said. His almost colorless eyes rested gently on Rye's face. "If I were you I wouldn't discuss that theory in public, Mr. Rye."

"I'll discuss it wherever I damned please," Rye said stubbornly. For the life of him he couldn't read beyond the mask which was Powers' face. "I'll make another little bet with you. The reason you're here this morning is to see how badly I want this other girl. She isn't lost; she isn't anywhere that you can't put a finger on her any time you want to." His teeth shone whitely in something that was not exactly a smile. "Well, the hell with her, and with you, too."

A little color had come into Powers' face, not much. "I'm afraid you'd lose that bet, Rye."

"Then I'll give you another," Rye said. He was on firmer ground now. Powers might know where Blossom Dee was. He did not know where Carmelita was. And though Rye himself was not sure that Carmelita had seen the announcement of Callahan's arrest, it was beginning to seem likely. The arrest would have frustrated her in whatever she meant to do. In a measure it would have assuaged her thirst for vengeance, though Rye was of the opinion that she would not be entirely satisfied until they had actually closed the door on a man named Edward Callahan. Why, then, had she run away? Obviously because Patterson Powers had tried to probe into her past. Not knowing his motives, not knowing that he had almost as much reason to hate the Callahan tribe as she had, she had feared a second trap and had vanished. "Because you found her with me, and hoped to use her as a lever to make me produce Gerald for you to cuff around, or worse, you tried to pump her." Rye regarded Joe without love. "As I recall her, she's a very sensitive girl. You scared her off."

Powers tried to keep the eagerness from his voice but was not entirely successful. "Who is she?"

"Just a girl," Rye said. He contrived a fairly lecherous leer. "I was giving her a build-up with Izzy Arnstein, and if you hadn't had to stick your nose in — "

Powers looked at the ceiling. "Nothing to do with this jam Callahan's in, eh?"

"Callahan isn't in any jam," Rye said. "He'll be out by two

o'clock this afternoon." He tossed the covers back and sat up, frankly exposing the gun. "I'll see you gentlemen to the door."

Joe said, "You son of a bitch."

Rye smiled at him. "It will give me a great deal of pleasure to kick your teeth in some day, Joey. Some time when I'm not barefooted." The gun in his fist indicated the door. "Out."

"I'd still like to see Gerald," Powers said evenly.

Rye nodded. "The first chance I get I'll tell him." He followed his guests across the living room, not too closely, for he had no illusions about either Powers or the gorilla Joe. He had good reason to remember how close Joe had come to killing him with but two blows. It was almost with relief that he saw El Segundo Ruiz standing there in the hall as his other guests departed. "Well, well, I've been expecting you!"

There was a brief moment in which Powers hesitated, studying Rye's latest visitor. Then with an abrupt nod he went on down the hall and joined Joe at the elevators. Ruiz looked from the retreating back to the gun in Rye's hand. He laughed his sly, fat laugh. "They do not like you, Señor."

"Nobody likes me," Rye said.

The fat man's gesture disparaged that. "Ah, but I like you, Señor. That is why I am here." Again he looked down the hall to where the elevator door was just closing. "They are perhaps interested in the same matter as you and I?"

Rye shook his head. "No." He stood aside and permitted Ruiz to enter the room. He closed the door and locked it.

Ruiz was unimpressed, either by the locked door or the gun. He sat, comfortably and appreciatively, in the room's most capacious chair. Using both hands he removed his black felt hat and placed it carefully on his fat black knees. "Guns are not for you and me, Señor." Fatly, slyly, his laugh crept around the walls. A shaft of sunlight gave his hair the look of oiled jet. "You will not shoot me, because then you would have to get rid of the body." His eyes twinkled. "And El Segundo's body, it is so very heavy, no?"

"Besides," Rye said, "you've probably got some friends downstairs who would worry about you."

Ruiz was delighted. "We understand each other, my friend." For a moment his happiness left him and he was sad. "On the other hand, I can not shoot you for you have something that I want."

Rye tossed the gun into a drawer. "Carmelita?"

"She would be of value," the fat man admitted. "She is not necessary."

"Oh?"

Fat, olive brown cheeks pushed El Segundo's eyes almost shut. "It is a matter of time only, you see. If Carmelita speaks, then Ruiz has nothing to sell." He sighed, rather pleasurably. "But if she speaks, then your friend Callahan must surely hang." He examined the tips of his large black shoes. "No, my friend, Carmelita is more your worry than mine."

"You're not exactly in the clear yourself," Rye pointed out. He looked at El Segundo's hands, trying to visualize them as the hands which had throttled an old lady who wore white tatting collars. He thought it was odd that the papers had given her death so little space. As yet they had not connected it with Callahan and the death of Lou Small. "Did you get my name from Mrs. Kampf or did you wait until the papers mentioned it?"

Ruiz opened his eyes very wide. "Ah, that poor lady!" His hands gently smoothed the nap of the hat on his knees. "That is another reason you should do business with El Segundo, my young friend. A word to the police might convince them it was you who killed her."

"Or you," Rye said.

Bulky shoulders moved the tight-fitting black coat in a faint shrug of distaste. "Is she so important, amigo? The important one is your friend Callahan, no? We must to save him further embarrassment, yes?"

Rye's eyes were clear and bright. "How much?"

Ruiz chuckled. "Now we come to the point, eh?" With a gesture oddly reminiscent of Callahan he smoothed the pendulous jowls which almost obscured his collar. "I now have two possible markets for my information. It has taken me a little time to understand the situation, but I believe that Señor Granger would pay well for a motive with which to prosecute Señor Callahan." He spread his hands. "But I am sympathize with Señor Callahan." He smiled. "So I offer him first chance."

"You don't have to sell me on the idea," Rye said. "I know what you've got." With his bare toes he scratched an itch on the opposite shin. "I asked you how much?"

Ruiz closed his eyes until they were mere slits. "Shall we say fifty — " He shook his head. "No, Ruiz will be generous. Twenty-five thousand dollars."

"By God," Rye said admiringly, "that is generous!" He appeared to think about that for a moment. "What would I get for the money? You have proof that Carmelita is his daughter?"

Ruiz was regretful. "Some scraps of letters written by her mother." And then, as he saw Rye's mouth tighten, his fat, sly laugh again crept around the room. "The letters are perhaps not proof, Señor, but in Mazatlan and Santa Caterina there will be those who remember."

"Yes," Rye said, "there is always that, isn't there?" He looked at his hands. "Naturally I don't carry that much money with me."

"Naturally."

"And besides, with the girl at large, your information may not be worth anything."

El Segundo's surprise was genuine. "Then you haven't her?"

"No." Rye began pacing the room. "She got away from me."

The fat man sat perfectly still for a long moment. His gross body was as immobile as Buddha carved in stone. Then words pushed his fat lips outward, not nice words. After a time he sighed. "If you are telling the truth, Señor, you must find her." He stood up. "As for me, that but shortens the time I can give you." He expelled a sibilant breath. "You yourself have said that if I wait — "

"She may already have spoken."

Ruiz compressed his thick lips. "I will go to Granger."

"He won't believe you if you can't produce the girl." Rye watched sweat break out on the fat man's forehead. "Why don't you help me find her?" He measured his next words carefully. "Tell you what I'll do. I'll have Callahan sprung by two o'clock. If she sees this morning's papers and then hears that he is free she may go to Granger herself — or to the police. Whichever one of us picks her up, the twenty-five grand is still good. You haven't got much, but you've got enough so that I can't afford to cross you."

Ruiz considered that. "But if Callahan is freed?"

"They can always arrest him again, can't they?" Rye drew a deep breath. "They will, too, the minute any new evidence turns up." His mouth made a stubborn line. "You'll have to take it or leave it. I won't lay out all that dough so long as there's a chance for her to beat you to the punch."

El Segundo's eyes got a cunning look. "Señor Granger may not be so cautious." He tried to see behind the mask which was Rye's face. Apparently he was not successful, or not sure of what he saw, for presently he sighed. "This will happen at two o'clock, you say?"

Rye nodded. "About that."

The fat man put on his hat, very carefully, using both hands and regarding the result in the mirror over the console. "Until two, then." He sighed again, heavily. "I am a patient man, Señor." He went out, swiftly and without even so much as looking back.

Rye went into the bedroom and began dressing. He was knotting a blue foulard tie over a paler blue shirt when there was another knock on the hall door. Thinking it was the boy after the breakfast tray he called a "Come in," and went on with his dressing. He was surprised when Earl Holly opened the door. Then, remembering, his eyes got that oddly muddy look again and he stared at the dapper, pink-cheeked young man as though he had never seen him before. "On your way, Earl. I don't want any part of you."

Holly licked his lips. "Now wait a minute, Bill — "

"Out."

Holly was apologetic but he could be as stubborn as the next man. He came in and closed the door. "All right, so I was a heel. I'm trying to make it up to you." And when Rye took a step toward him: "God damn it, do you want to see the girl or don't you?"

Rye just stood there for an instant, neither believing nor disbelieving. "Am I to understand you know where she is?"

Holly nodded. "That's right."

"And you're telling me about it? Why?"

"Because I thought maybe you'd like to know," Holly said. "The jam Callahan is in and one thing and another — Well, I got to thinking and — "

Rye buttoned his coat. "How'd you happen to find her?"

Holly fumbled around with that one for a while. When finally he lifted his eyes they were embarrassed but honest. "You probably won't understand this, but I kind of like that babe. There's something about her — " He shrugged his plump well-tailored shoulders. "Well, anyway, I saw her go out with Powers and that gorilla of his, and later on I went back and talked to Izzy Arnstein. That brought me to Powers' Orchid Club along about one o'clock this morning, just in time to see her come out the back way."

"You talk to her?"

"No."

"Well, what in hell did you do?"

"She's in a hole-in-the-wall hotel on Spring Street. I think's she's sick."

"So you came to me," Rye said stonily.

Holly's face whitened. "I can always leave."

Rye went into the bedroom and got a hat. "All right, let's go." They went out and down to the basement garage. All the way downtown neither man said anything. There was a stiffness between them that would take a little time to completely eradicate. No doubt Holly felt that on his part he had done all he could to rectify the mistake which was his. Rye himself always found it difficult to see friendships in anything but sharp blacks and whites. Gradations, shadows, were something you had to expect in your enemies; if you had to look for it in your friends too, then where was the difference?

As Holly had said, the place was a hole in the wall. Between a not-too-inviting sandwich shop and a cut-rate stationery store narrow glass doors gave on a narrow stairway leading up to a gloomy region described by a sign which read: "Rooms, Transient." Rye remembered with a shock how little Money Carmelita had had of her own. He remembered too the exactness with which she had replaced every stitch his money, or Callahan's, had bought.

They went up the stairs, past a glassed-in cubicle like a sentry box, empty now, and along a hall made up of blank doors and smells and gloom. Holly paused before one of the doors, nodding that this was it. Though there seemed no particular need for quiet, both men acted as though stealth were necessary. Beyond the paper-thin door there was the creak of bedsprings, and a faint snuffling sound, like a very small, very unhappy puppy. Rye tested the doorknob gently, pulling it toward him so that there would be no tell-tale click. The door was locked. After a while he knelt and examined the keyhole, found it empty and made motions behind his back. Holly put a dime-store pass key into his hand. Presently Rye opened the door.

She lay diagonally across the sagging bed, face down, fully dressed in the familiar cheap little outfit. Around and about her were crumpled newspapers. One of the headlines stared up at Rye: GOVERNOR'S FRIEND AND BACKER ARRESTED FOR MURDER! He went in and closed the door quietly behind him. When he came out again, some fifteen minutes later, his dark skin had a yellowish cast and his eyes were harried. "All right, Earl, you can go in now." He went swiftly, unseeingly, down the dingy hall.

CHAPTER 16

THE general offices of Calexico Oil seemed to be functioning about as usual, though there was a little hush as Rye went through, almost as if the rank and file were ashamed to be caught working when their chief executive languished in jail. In the anteroom which was part of Callahan's own private suite Sherry McKay was also pretending to conduct business as usual. The pile of opened wires on her desk, however, and the trend of her remarks into the two hot phones, indicated that politics had temporarily superseded oil. Rye picked up one of the wires. It was from a man in the extreme southern part of the state, assuring Callahan of his continued support and offering condolences. It was noteworthy that this man had never been able to deliver more than fifty votes. Some of the other wires were not so pleasant. Rye's lean brown fingers stacked them all neatly and replaced them exactly as he had found them. "Good morning, Sherry."

She leaned back and regarded him with the look which always made him wish he had led a better life. The mahogany glints in her dark hair were quite noticeable. As nearly as he could tell without

Dig Me A Grave

meeting them directly her eyes were gray. "How are you feeling this morning?"

"Lumpy," he admitted, still avoiding her eyes. Almost diffidently he said, "About last night — "

"You were insufferable!"

He looked at her then. "Because I was doing my job?"

The color in her cheeks heightened a trifle. "It's a dirty job, Bill. Lying and chicane and — and bribery — " She leaned forward and snapped the switch that deadened the ringing phones. "I suppose I'm like the owner of property he knows is being used for immoral purposes. As long as it isn't brought right out into the open — when you don't make me an actual party to it — " She thrust her chair back and stood up and went to the windows. "Damn it, I tried to call you this morning, to tell you I was sorry I'd walked out on you." She turned and faced him. "There was something in me that — well, I just couldn't do it, that's all."

His eyes, his mouth, were faintly amused. "And this is the girl who bopped a cop last night. With a brick."

"That was different."

He shook his head. "No it wasn't. It's all part of the same thing — a game, if you like." He thought about that, quite earnestly, because sometimes he felt a little bit as Sherry did. "Not always a nice game, perhaps, but stimulating." He lit a cigarette for her and presently one for himself. "Besides, there's Callahan. I told you how I felt about him." And when she answered nothing to that he said, "What's bothering you is what's bothering a lot of people — the same thing that's always bothered them. You don't see the necessity for lying and chicane in politics. To be quite frank with you, I don't, either. All I know is that the people themselves don't seem to want complete honesty. They're ready to believe the worst of every man who sticks his head up above the mob, and so long as that is true you've got to use the same tactics the opposition does." He stared intently at the tip of his cigarette. "You don't think Weldon Granger is interested in the good of the people, do you?"

She made an impatient gesture. "Is Callahan? Is Quarrie?"

He flushed. "This state is getting as good a run for its money as any. Better than most."

"And Callahan's interest is purely altruistic?"

"No."

"That's what I mean," she said tiredly.

He came and put a hand under her chin. "All this is beside the point, Sherry. If I give you my word that Callahan did not commit those — that murder, will you do something for me?" He took to pacing the room. "What you said last night about my playing God — well, I've reached the place where I need help. There's a girl — you saw her last night — a rather bewildered little girl who needs your help even more than I do. I can't go to Sybil with her because — " He drew a deep breath. "All right, I can't expect you to stumble around in the dark." Briefly he told her about Carmelita and Callahan, and about El Segundo Ruiz. "I'm not offering anything in extenuation except the fact that the minute Callahan learned about her he was ready to risk a large part of what he's got to make it up to her. He has risked it. Foolishly, perhaps, but there it is."

She remained perfectly quiet for a moment. "Your word of honor that Callahan isn't — that he didn't — "

Rye forced himself to stare straight into the doubt-filled eyes. "Word of honor, Sherry."

"Then I'll go see her." She crossed to a closet and got her hat and coat and bag. "God help you if you're lying to me, Bill."

"I'm not," he assured her. At the door he put an arm around her and kissed her briefly. "You're a grand person, Miss McKay. Maybe I'll reform one of these days, just for you." He watched her down the hall. After a time, plucking thoughtfully at his lower lip, he went along the short lateral corridor to the legal department and entered Harris Friedlander's office.

Friedlander had a copy of the *Chronicle* spread out on his desk. His dark handsome face wore a frown as Rye came in. He erased it. "I see you pulled it off."

Rye closed the door and leaned his back against it. "Yes." He was conscious that his clothes, though probably costing as much as Friedlander's did not look as well. "Knebel has altered his records to show that a man named Callahan called on him last month to have a twisted ankle taped up. It was then that Callahan must have left the fingerprints on the stair walls. Knebel assures me that the walls haven't been washed in years, so that ought to stand up."

"I still don't like it," Friedlander said.

Rye went on in a carefully emotionless voice. "Dr. Knebel recalled the incident the minute he saw Callahan's picture in the papers. Because my name had previously been associated with Callahan's" — he thought it was odd that Granger's spite-prompted squib should have been of value after all — "Knebel called me and I passed the information on to the *Chronicle*."

Friedlander pursed his lips. "Suppose the police try to break him down."

"They may try," Rye said. "He understands that they may." He looked at the carnation in Friedlander's buttonhole. "There are several reasons why they won't succeed. He's signed a paper which I have, stating that he was willing to perjure himself. Even if the cops offered him leniency I could force a conviction with that."

"Convicting yourself too," Friedlander said drily. He clipped the end from a thin dappled cigar. "Not that that would do Knebel much good." He studied Rye with faintly antagonistic eyes. "Mind telling me the other reasons?"

"He's still short eight of the ten thousand I promised him," Rye said. He looked at his hand and saw that it was trembling slightly. "There's a third reason that we needn't go into right now."

"I see."

"No, you don't," Rye said carefully. "All you see is that now there is almost a total lack of incriminating evidence against your client. The gun is palpably a frame. You can go before any magistrate and demand — if not a release — at least nominal bail." He turned and opened the door. "I'd appreciate it if you could learn whether it was a man or woman who phoned in that anonymous tip."

Friedlander's voice halted him, sharply. "Rye — did Callahan do it?"

"No."

"How do you know?"

"Because I did it," Rye said. He went out.

It was almost noon when Rye entered the office building directly opposite his own. A lot of early lunchers were going into Granger's

Cafeteria No. 1, under the giant banner which said: NOW LET'S CLEAN UP THE STATE! At the lobby cigar stand some men were arguing with the clerk over the payoff on a punchboard. There was no secrecy about it. Weldon Granger's newly elected mayor and district attorney apparently thought there was no use in being too clean. Rye bought some cigarettes and leaned on the showcase for a moment, examining the crowded street for a sign of El Segundo Ruiz. There wasn't any. Presently an elevator carried him up to the executive offices of Granger's Cafeterias, Incorporated, and he had only a short wait before being admitted to the august presence of Mr. Weldon Granger himself.

"Well, well, Mr. Rye!" Granger affected extreme affability. His full, cherry-red lips smiled a welcome and he was literally bursting with the milk of human kindness. The office was severely plain, as befitted a man who wouldn't live in the lap of luxury while the masses starved. "What can I do for you?"

Rye carefully examined all the doors and windows. There was a furtive air about him. A green bead of light glowed on the annunciator at Mr. Granger's elbow, indicating an open switch. Rye went over and closed it. Mr. Granger frowned. Rye said in a conspirator's whisper, "We wouldn't want our conversation transcribed, would we?"

Eyes like large blue marbles had a little difficulty concealing their owner's eagerness. "I assure you I don't know what you're talking about, Mr. Rye."

"I'm talking about twenty-five thousand dollars."

Granger's triple chins rested on his shirt front. "A large sum."

"But not too large," Rye said. "Not for something that would throw Callahan back in jail — this time for keeps." His mouth was thin and hard. "You knew they were springing him, didn't you?"

Granger nodded. "I thought it possible." He pursed his lips. "Just what is your interest in the matter?"

"Twenty-five grand," Rye said.

"And what else?"

"Does there have to be something else?" Rye went to the door opening on the public corridor and peered out. When he closed it and again faced Granger there was angry resentment in his eyes.

"I've been with Callahan a long time, licking his boots, doing his dirty work. I'm fed up with it. This latest caper of his has come a little too close, even for me, and I'm not going to put my neck in a sling for the kind of dough he's paying me." His mouth twitched. "You offered to buy something. I've got it to sell."

Granger tried to look unimpressed. "Such as?"

Rye licked his lips. "The motive the police haven't been able to find."

"You're leaving Callahan?"

"Not necessarily." A slow flush darkened Rye's skin. He hoped it would be misunderstood by his inquisitor. His ears were straining for some sign of El Segundo's arrival. He was a little surprised that the fat man had waited even this long. "I'm just not going to be able to cover up for him, that's all. He moved restlessly, nervously, about the office. "Gerald and Sybil will inherit when he's gone. I can handle them without so much grief."

The callousness of that remark was almost too much, even for Weldon Granger. His rubicund face paled. "How do I — how can I be sure that — ?"

"That I'm not crossing you?" Rye laughed unpleasantly. "I'll take a check. If my information isn't worth anything to you, you can always stop the check, can't you?"

"By God!" Granger said. He reminded himself that even in emergencies he must be careful of such expressions. "By Heavens — " A thin veil of caution glazed his eyes. "All right, I'm listening. What was his motive?"

Rye shook his head. "The check first."

"Now, see here, Mr. Rye, if I had any intentions of — ah — of not playing fair with a shrewd person like you, why I'd — "

"The check first," Rye repeated stubbornly.

Sighing, Granger got out some check books. He had a little trouble deciding which account to use. Finally settling on one, he filled in the date, the amount. "Whom shall I make it out to?"

"Ruiz," Rye said. He watched the bland, pink-skinned face. There was surprise, but no evidence that Granger had associated the name with anything recent. "El Segundo Ruiz."

Granger filled in the line and signed his name with a flourish.

"An odd alias, Mr. Rye."

"I've got lots of them," Rye said. He was attacked with a fit of sneezing, so that it was natural for him to have a handkerchief in his hand when he accepted the check and stowed it in his billfold.

Mr. Granger eyed him expectantly. "Now!"

"Now," Rye said, "now, Mr. Weldon Granger, you can go to hell." He moved without hurry to the outside door. Behind him there was a stunned silence. Then Granger's swivel chair made a tremendous racket, and Granger's voice was yelling, "So it was a trick! I'll have you jailed, I'll — I'll stop the check!"

"I told you you could, didn't I?" With a hand on the knob Rye turned and looked at the irate man. "I didn't expect to cash it, pal. I just wanted to see how far you'd go." He smiled pleasantly and went out, closing the door gently behind him. Down the corridor he saw El Segundo Ruiz just getting out of an elevator. At the same moment Ruiz saw Rye. Because he was two hours early, because he couldn't understand Rye's being there at all, it was perfectly obvious to him that the whole business was a trap. His elephantine bulk moved with incongruous agility. At the same instant that his foot went backward and blocked the closing elevator doors he produced a pistol and pointed it at Rye. The elevator boy instinctively released the air and the doors banged open. Ruiz backed inside. The doors slammed. Above them, the indicator hand almost bent itself double in the effort to reach the numeral 1.

Rye descended the stairs without haste. When he reached the lobby there was quite a crowd around the chattering, gesticulating elevator boy. Ruiz was not a part of it. He had evaporated.

CHAPTER 17

ON the steps of City Hall Callahan and Sybil and Harris Friedlander posed briefly for the news photographers. Callahan was restrained. Sybil, very beautiful in black, clung to her husband's arm and wept prettily for the cameras. Friedlander was the assured, competent attorney who had never been worried over the outcome at all. Not really. It was quite an event.

From a drug store across the street, where he had been keeping a wary eye open for El Segundo Ruiz, Rye watched the little procession descend the rest of the steps to the street level, where Sybil's chauffeur-driven town car waited. There was a fair crowd, made up mostly of Hall attaches and those who had business at the Hall. Oddly, there was not a single policeman in evidence. Rye crossed over in the pedestrian zone. "Hello, Ed. Hello, Sybil — Fried." Though he did not smile, his face was smooth and untroubled.

"Hello, Bill," Callahan said. The others said hello. A reporter from the *Post-Express*, puffing, because he had been late for the triumphal exit and had had to chase all the way down the steps, asked Callahan for a statement. "What about the gun?"

Callahan eyed him. "Why don't you ask Granger?"

The man retired in obvious confusion. Friedlander helped Sybil into the tonneau. As Callahan was about to follow, Rye laid a hand on his arm. "Ed."

"Yes?"

"Let Fried and Sybil go on. There's something I've got to talk to you about." Rye flagged down a passing yellow cab. He looked at Sybil. "Mind?"

Now that there was no longer any real need for her tears Sybil had stopped crying. "What are you trying to do, be funny? The only reason I'm here is that Ed and Fried thought it would look well."

Callahan remained poker-faced. "Thank you, Sybil."

Rye watched Friedlander get in beside her. "No news of Gerald yet?"

She shook her head. "He hasn't been home. He may have called up, I don't know. Van Sweringen would know." The car rolled smoothly away.

Rye and Callahan got into the cab and Rye gave the man the address of a fifth-rate hotel on Spring Street. Callahan rolled down the windows and sniffed appreciatively at the warm fresh air. Sunlight made his skin ruddy. He said, "I'll remember this, Bill."

"Forget it."

Almost furtively Callahan studied Rye's profile. "What are you sore about?"

"Because we're not out of the woods yet. I've managed to confuse Ruiz for a moment, but it won't last."

"And Carmelita?"

"I've got her," Rye said. "Earl Holly found her for me — partly for himself too — and I had a talk with her this morning. He drew a careful breath. "She's taken quite a beating, Ed — all this running around. She's emotionally upset." He watched the two o'clock traffic of which the cab was a part. "Ever think that you could adopt her, Ed?"

Callahan was startled. "With Sybil around?"

"I'll take care of Sybil," Rye said. He had not made up his mind just how he would do this, but it would have to be done. "I can't think of any other way you can give her the name she's entitled to."

Callahan's breathing was labored. "And what does Carmelita say to that?"

"I haven't mentioned it to her. I've been busy trying to whitewash you, not only for walking out on her mother, but for a couple of murders she thinks you did." He watched Callahan's hands. They were motionless.

Callahan's voice was as dry as corn husks. "A couple you said? Who was the other one?"

"A Mrs. Kampf. Carmelita's ex-landlady." Rye half turned in the seat. "Where were you last night, Ed — say around eight o'clock?"

Callahan's eyes were bleak. The muscles along his jaw line were rigid with repression. "So it's like that!"

"It's like that," Rye said. "I've got to know, Ed."

"Suppose I don't choose to tell you? Suppose I lied?"

"I'd still have to find out, Ed."

Callahan pretended to be interested in his nails. His square strong fingers were white at the knuckles. "I don't think we can be very good friends after this, Bill."

"All right." Rye's face was expressionless.

Quite suddenly Callahan laughed. "You're a fool. Why should I have killed your precious old lady?"

Rye stiffened. "How do you know she was an old lady? I didn't say so."

"The papers did."

"Yes," Rye said presently. "Yes, that's right, isn't it?"

The cab pulled into a red zone and he got out and paid off. "All right, we'll forget that for a moment and see how you get along with the girl. A lot depends on that."

They went up the narrow stairs, past the little cubbyhole of an office, set like a sentry box at the head. The cubicle was still empty, or again. A small cardboard sign set beside the old-fashioned tap bell said that if you wanted the manager you could ring for him. Pale gray illumination sifted through the frosted glass of an overhead skylight. Callahan's breathing was noisy in the stillness. All the ruddiness was gone from his face and the eagerness in his eyes was belied by his lagging steps. He looked like a sick man.

As they came to the door Rye put a hand on the older man's arm. It was trembling. With his free hand he tapped lightly on the panel. There was no sound from within. Impatiently now, and louder, he rapped again, and then, getting no answer, his face suddenly white and strained, he twisted the knob and thrust the door violently inward. Sherry McKay lay face down on the floor, motionless. Except for her the room was empty. There was no sign of either Earl Holly or Carmelita.

Callahan's hoarse cry sounded as though it had been torn from him. "Christ!"

"Be quiet," Rye said. Even before he went and knelt at Sherry's side he made sure the door was closed and latched securely. Sherry was not dead. Indeed at first it appeared that she was only asleep. Then exploring fingers found a swelling bruise at the base of her skull. Rye lifted her and carried her to the bed. "Get some water," he directed Callahan.

After a time the limp figure stirred of its own violition, and Sherry's eyes came open, unwillingly, afraid of what they might see. They stared at Rye as if he were an utter stranger. Then the blankness went out of them and she struggled up in his arms. "Bill, did they — have they — ?" Frantically her eyes searched the room, saw Callahan without acknowledging his presence, saw that what she was looking for was not there. She shuddered violently and began to retch.

"Stop it!" Rye said sharply.

Someone knocked on the door. Rye freed himself and straightened, looked at the door, finally took up a position beside it and motioned Callahan to answer the knock.

Earl Holly came in. Surprise widened his blue eyes as he recognized Callahan. Then, very swiftly, he took in the scene and what he conceived to be the reason for it. His right hand disappeared beneath his coat. "I might have expected something like this." His gun was clear of the shoulder clip when Rye chopped down on the wrist above it. They struggled together for a moment. Instinctively Callahan bent and picked up the fallen gun. He did not seem to know what to do with it.

"Be still, Earl," Rye said. His long arm encompassed the smaller man's plump body. "This isn't what you think."

"The hell it isn't!"

Sherry sat up on the bed. "Earl!"

Rye let him go then. "Aren't things bad enough without you blowing your top?" He was breathing angrily, gustily, through his nose when he closed the door and leaned his back against it. "Where the hell have you been?"

"I went out for a bite to eat," Holly said sullenly. And then in a tight furious voice he demanded of Sherry: "What happened? At least, let's have your version of what happened." It was obvious that he still thought it was a plant, and that she was a party to it.

Sherry's face was white, but she kept her voice carefully matter-of-fact. "Someone knocked. I thought it was you coming back. I unlocked the door, opened it, saw no one there and foolishly stuck my head out." She shrugged. "That's all I remember, except for a lot of fireworks."

"It makes a good story," Holly sneered.

Rye said, "That's enough of that, Earl. If we'd wanted the girl out of the way we could have taken care of her long ago."

"Except that you didn't know where she was." Holly's voice was bitter. "It took me to tell you." He brushed a hand over his eyes. "My God, what a sap!"

Callahan's face was the color of skimmed milk. "Who — ?"

"I don't know," Rye said. "I've got ideas, maybe, but I don't know for sure." He stared intently at Sherry. "Could anybody have followed you this morning?"

She shrugged. "It's possible. I didn't see anyone?"

Rye looked questioningly at the room's one window. "Could she have signalled anyone?"

"No." Sherry shook her head. "She wouldn't have — " Her eyes went to Callahan's face. "His picture in the papers, the fact that he was in trouble, must have done something to her. She was almost — "

Holly's extreme youth and the way he himself felt about Carmelita were evident in the bitterness of his words. "Sure, we softened her up for you all right. We practically painted a halo around Callahan's head."

Callahan growled deep down in his throat. His big strong hands curled a little at his sides, as though eager to fasten into something, anything, from which he could wrest relief. There was sweat on his upper lip. "Well, Bill?"

"I don't know," Rye said. He looked at Holly. "If you're all through sulking I could use you."

"Doing what?"

"Helping me keep track of Granger."

"You think Granger's responsible for this?"

"Not directly, no." Rye's mouth made a firm hard line. "I do think he's our best bet to locate Ruiz, though. Ruiz isn't stopped. He's only been delayed." He told them about the fat man's attempted visit to Granger's office. "I'd hoped to get a line on him through a friend of mine in Little Mexico, but it hasn't worked out that way. We'll have to do the next best thing." He looked at Sherry. "Mind if Callahan takes you home, hon?"

Callahan demurred. "There must be something I can do besides that." He apologized to Sherry. "Not that I don't appreciate all you've done, McKay, but — " His glance included Holly. "You too, son."

"The hell with you," Holly said. "What I've done, if any, hasn't been for your sake. I hate your guts."

Callahan flushed. "I'm sorry you feel that way, son."

Rye said, "What Holly doesn't appreciate is that we're all on the same side — now." He was oppressed with the knowledge that it was still a one-man show. He did not believe that it was El Segundo Ruiz who had the girl. While it was possible for Ruiz to have picked him up at the office, and later followed Sherry from the office here, it was unlikely that Ruiz could have known her well enough to realize the connection. But if he told Holly this, or Callahan either, they were almost sure to go off chasing Carmelita instead of Ruiz, who was by far the more imminent danger. "The Mexican will not try to contact us any more. His attempted double-cross this morning will make that unfeasible. He will not go to the police, because there would be no profit in that. Granger is his best bet, and ours."

"All right," Holly said sullenly. "Do I take the house or the office?"

"The house," Rye decided. He looked at his watch. "If nothing happens I'll see you out there." He turned and went swiftly from the room.

Darkness had fallen and Seventh Street was a swift-flowing river of traffic between neon-lit canyon walls when at a few minutes past six Weldon Granger emerged from the building. He was in a hurry, but apparently he was not going far, for he neither used his own car, parked with political license beside a fire plug, nor did he hail a cab. His hat and topcoat were faintly reminiscent of William Jennings Bryan.

Rye trailed along without difficulty, keeping a few people between them, not too many. He had waited too long to risk either losing his man or being discovered. At Broadway Granger waited for the change of lights, crossed over and waited again for the North-and-South change. Because he was afraid of closing the gap without a reasonable margin of safety, Rye chose to skip the cross signal and parallel Granger's course on the opposite side of the street. Thus when he entered the Hotel Lancaster he was perhaps a minute or a minute and a half behind Granger and was just in time to see that gentleman's coat tails vanishing into an up elevator.

There was quite a crowd at the desk. It did not seem possible that Granger had made an inquiry there. Obviously, then, he must know exactly where he was going, which was more than Rye did. Rye crossed over to an alcove under the main staircase and found Sam McLoughlin at his desk. McLoughlin was the Lancaster's house man. "Hello, Sam." Rye was in a terrific hurry now, because this thing had to be timed almost to a gnat's eyebrow. "I hate to tear you away from that chair, but I think you're going to have a little trouble upstairs."

McLoughlin looked at him from beneath an overhang of steel-wool brows. "You wouldn't be kidding an old man, would you?"

Rye shook his head. "If I am, the drinks are on me, Sam." He watched Granger's elevator come down. "You've got a big fat Mexican staying here. Name of Ruiz, the last I heard of him." He was relieved when McLoughlin conceded this to be a fact. There had been the possibility that it wasn't Ruiz whom Granger was visiting. "The guy who just went up to see him isn't a particular friend of mine. Just the same I'd hate to have anything happen to him."

McLoughlin got to his feet. "This Ruiz is bad, hunh?"

"Bad," Rye agreed. "For a fat man he's about the fastest thing with a gun I've ever seen."

McLoughlin patted the bulge under his left lapel. "Let's go up."

In the fifth floor corridor Rye said, "I'll go in first, Sam, but you'll have to back me up. I haven't got a gun."

McLoughlin nodded. "Who's the party with him?"

"Granger."

McLoughlin pursed his lips in a whistle that was eloquent without being noisy. "Like that, hunh?" Soft carpet muffled their footsteps. The corridor was deserted. The house dick paused before a door marked 551, pointing. Rye bent an ear to the panel. He could hear voices inside, could not hear what was being said. With his right hand he put a firm tension on the knob, pulling the door to him until he had released the catch. Then, very quickly, he went in.

Ruiz was sitting on the edge of the bed, his great weight depressing the springs till the mattress looked like a V. Facing him, hands and hat on his knees, Weldon Granger was a one-man senate investigating committee getting an earful. Both men looked up as the door opened. Ruiz was the only one that moved. His fat brown right hand had the swiftness of light as it disappeared beneath his coat, came out with the pistol. Rye threw out an arm and fell in the opposite direction. A red-hot poker scorched his arm. There was the sound of a shot. Then, very loud, there were two more shots. He raised himself to an elbow and looked at Sam McLoughlin bulking large in the doorway. "Thanks, Sam."

Weldon Granger had fainted.

El Segundo Ruiz was on his hands and knees looking for a gun he could not see. Blood ran out of a hole in his throat and dripped to the carpet. Presently he got tired of looking and fell on his face. There was another hole that gaped widely in his back. One of McLoughlin's bullets had come out that way. McLoughlin said, "You shouldn't ought to have made me done that, Bill." He turned and looked at the gathering crowd in the corridor. "Just keep your heads, folks. Nothing more is going to happen." He came in and closed the door and locked it.

Rye was bending over Ruiz with a handkerchief in his hand. "Dead," he said. He stood up, pushing his left coat- and shirt-sleeve far back to expose a shallow bleeding furrow in his left forearm. He used the handkerchief to stop some of the bleeding. "You've got a nice eye, Sam." His face was smooth and unworried.

"Too nice," McLoughlin grumbled. He went to the phone.

Weldon Granger opened his eyes. "Wha— what happened?" He saw Ruiz on the floor and was sick. Rye let him be sick and began opening dresser drawers, quickly but noiselessly. Sam McLoughlin was talking to somebody at Police Headquarters. Rye did not find anything that shouldn't be found.

After a while Granger quit being sick and stood up and tried to go out the door. McLoughlin put out an arm thick and rigid as a loading boom and stopped him. "Be quiet, you." He went on talking into the telephone. "Send a squad around with the wagon, *pronto*."

Granger mopped at his face with a pale lavender-bordered handkerchief. From behind it his bulgy blue eyes appraised Rye's face. "How — how did you get here?"

"I followed you," Rye said. With his teeth and one hand he finished knotting the impromptu tourniquet about his forearm. The arm was beginning to hurt now, a little, not much. He thought it was a cheap price to pay for what he had accomplished. He wished he could have had a few more minutes with Ruiz's things. "He give you anything you could use?"

Fear came into Granger's eyes, then anger, then fear again. "If I said yes, I suppose you and your hired thug would kill me too?"

McLoughlin cradled the phone. "Nobody hires me to do things like that." He hit Granger in the mouth. Granger retired whimpering to a chair and sat in it, trying not to look at the black-clothed body on the floor. McLoughlin sat on the bed and looked moodily at Rye. "You shouldn't ought to have made me done that," he said again.

Rye was furious. "I didn't make you do anything. I just told you what you were going up against."

McLoughlin shook his head. "You only told me part of it." He sighed. "I better know the other parts before the cops come."

From the corner of his eye Rye watched Granger's face. "It's all tied in with this frame against Callahan. I'm not saying that Granger had a hand in it, understand, but Ruiz either had something to sell or was pretending that he had." He tried to pull his coat-sleeve down over the makeshift bandage. "I first noticed this fat guy when the cops took me down to look at Lou Small. He was part of the crowd. Later — around noon today — I ran into him again outside of Granger's office. He yanked a gun and got away."

Granger's voice was a hoarse frightened croak. "Young man, are you insinuating that I had anything to do with — ?"

Rye appealed to McLoughlin. "Have I insinuated anything? I'm just telling you what happened."

Some cops came in. One of them was Lieutenant Nick Belarski. His sallow face, the bloodstreaked yellow of his eyeballs, looked as though he'd been losing a lot of sleep. "Now what's this?" he demanded. He carefully avoided looking directly at Rye. A couple of other cops came and looked at Ruiz. Presently they got down on their hands and knees beside him. Rye held his breath.

In a voice devoid of inflection Sam McLoughlin recounted exactly what had happened. He neither tried to shield himself nor Rye. "The guy had a gun. He used it. I let him have it."

Belarski held a hand out, palm up, to Rye. "Gun?"

"I haven't any," Rye said. He watched one of the detectives take a check out of El Segundo's pocket. He looked away. "McLoughlin told you what happened. That's the way it happened."

Granger let out a yelp as the detective got up and thrust the check at him. "Yours?" Granger's skin got the color of very old, very coarse wrapping paper. He turned accusing, anguished eyes on Rye's face. "You — you — !" He could not go on.

Some legmen from the police beat opened the door. Belarski yelled at them. "Out!" A couple of uniformed cops wrestled them back into the hall. Belarski looked at Rye. "Tell it again," he commanded. His thin lips writhed with the effort not to say anything else.

Rye repeated the story. "I'm not saying Granger hired him. I'm not saying he didn't. All I know is that the Callahan job looked like a plant, and I couldn't think of anybody else that would profit by that kind of a frame, so I kind of kept an eye on the opposition."

Granger stood up. "That is the damndest lie I ever heard. You know very well that you — that I — " He forced himself to look at Belarski. "Mr. Rye tricked me into giving him that check — this noon, in my office."

Rye neither denied nor affirmed this. He said, "Did I also trick you into coming here to meet him?"

Belaski snatched the check, looked at it, looked at Sam McLoughlin, jerked his head at the corpse. "His name Ruiz?"

"Unh-hunh."

Weldon Granger sat down as though all the strength had gone out of his legs. "Then that was part of — the trick!" He lifted eyes glazed like the patina on very old china to Belarski's face. "I give you my word I didn't know the man's name until this very moment. I — He telephoned me, suggesting a meeting." He drew a quivery, blubbery breath. "All I had was the room number."

"You're ready to swear it was Rye you gave the check to?"

"Yes!"

Belarski suddenly realized that the check was getting a lot of unnecessary fingerprints on it. He folded a handkerchief over it. "Proof?"

Again the uncertain, frightened look came into Granger's blue eyes. "I — don't know. I have witnesses that Rye called on me."

"But not that you gave him the check?"

"No."

Belarski glared at Rye. "What was the purpose of that call?"

"I'd rather not say until I know what I'm being accused of." Rye was polite, unworried. "As it stands now, Mr. Granger had an appointment with a man I believed to be dangerous. I happened to know of — or guess at — that appointment." He shrugged. "Who knows, I may even have saved Mr. Granger's life."

"Big-hearted Rye!" Belarski sneered. He turned to Sam McLoughlin. "You'll go into court with that story you handed us?"

"I won't like it." McLoughlin said heavily. He was still angry with Rye for having been made a party to what everybody — or nearly everybody — knew was a frame. "I won't like it, but I'll go." He stood up. "I'll tell it just like it happened. It's the truth."

"Your part of it, maybe."

"That's the only part I can do anything about," McLoughlin said. He went stolidly, without hurry, to the door. "If you need me I'll be down in my office." He went out.

Rye said tentatively, "Well, if there's nothing else I can do — " He held up his bandaged arm and moved toward the door.

Belarski blocked his way. "We're going down to the Hall."

"I don't want to go down to the Hall."

"That's all right," Belarski said. "A lot of people go down there that don't want to." His smile was suddenly wolfish. 'There's something come up in connection with another little matter you might be interested in."

Rye's stomach muscles quivered but his face remained placid. "I'll bet you had another anonymous phone call."

"Unh hunh." Belarski looked around, inviting his audience to share in the fun. "And what do you think this one was about?"

"I haven't the slightest idea," Rye said. He had a very good idea, but admitting it was not likely to do him any good. "Not the slightest."

"Then I'll tell you," Belarski said. "It's about the murder of an old lady named Mrs. Kampf. Remember her?"

"I never heard of her." Almost instantly Rye realized that he had made a mistake. Belarski's next words confirmed that impression. "There's some people down at the Hall think different. They're waiting to meet you."

CHAPTER 18

EXCEPT for its refined appointments Inspector Cain's outer office looked like the anteroom of an employment agency. There were a lot of people sitting around. Notable among them was the rather frowzy blonde whom El Segundo Ruiz had knocked cold in the hall of Mrs. Kampf's rooming house. Rye thought he recognized some of the others as tenants of the same place. He hoped his own face was as unrecognizable to them as theirs were to him.

Inspector Cain was his polite, restrained self; a chief of detectives who looked like a cleric. Floyd Ingram, the district attorney, had lost some of his bombast and appeared embarrassed rather than otherwise in the presence of a prisoner who was the man who had got him elected. Though Granger had not been formally arrested, his detention, even as a material witness, was a source of annoyance to the prosecutor. Granger had recovered a little of his customary aplomb, not much.

Belarski had the feverish look of a triumphant ferret. He pushed Rye toward the blonde. "Is this him?"

Rye said with an air of great surprise, "Why, hello, there! How's your head?"

He could just as well have thrown a bomb in Belarski's face. The blonde's too. Expecting him to deny everything, they were momentarily thrown off balance. Belarski was the first to recover. "I thought you'd never heard of her!"

"Is she the Mrs. Kampf you asked me about?" Rye shook his head. "No, obviously that's impossible. You said Mrs. Kampf had been murdered."

The blonde licked her lips. She look at Belarski. She said, "Well, what the hell, if he admits he was there — "

"Shut up!" Belarski snarled. He glared at his other witnesses, utterly useless to him now. Rye did not glare at them, but he studied them. It seemed to him that they were an odd assortment of roomers for Mrs. Kampf to have had. They did not quite fit in with the atmosphere of white tatting collars and Gideon Bibles.

Inspector Cain looked at Rye. "Am I to understand that you don't read the newspapers?"

"I've been pretty busy," Rye said. He aped Cain's manner. "Am I to understand that the landlady I talked to out there is the Mrs. Kampf who was murdered?"

Belarski pounced. "So you admit you talked to her!"

"Why, of course," Rye said. He explained for Cain's benefit. I've already told Lieutenant Belarski that I was interested in this Ruiz. I tailed him to the vicinity of the Westlake rooming house and was making some inquiries when — " He smiled sympathetically at the blonde. "You ought to remember him. He was the fat man you said hit you."

She remembered the fat man. She remembered him loudly and profanely. She said, "I'll bet it was him knocked the old gal off."

Belarski cursed her. "Well, for Christ's sake, why didn't you say that before?"

"Maybe you didn't ask her," Rye suggested pleasantly. He turned sultry eyes on Cain. "These anonymous tips you've been getting are just a little too pat to be relied on. If Belarski wasn't so intent on pinning something on me he might be able to think better." He pointed a finger at Belarski's nose. "Isn't it true that you went out there and asked all these good people if they'd seen a guy like me around? Did you ask 'em about anything else? Did you ask 'em about Ruiz, for instance?"

"I didn't even know about Ruiz!" Belarski yelled.

Rye spread his hands. "Well, there you are."

Inspector Cain pinched his lower lip between thumb and forefinger. "Maybe we're all losing sight of something pertinent here." His eyes massaged Rye's face. "There was a young lady staying with Mrs. Kampf. Oddly enough she seems to have borne a striking resemblance to the so-called mystery girl we were looking for in connection with the murder of Lou Small."

Cain looked at the blonde and her fellow roomers. "All right, you can go now. Thank you for coming down. If we need you again we'll let you know." He thought of something. "Would you mind stopping at the morgue on your way out? Lieutenant Belarski will show you the way. We'd like to get an identification on a man who was just killed."

Floyd Ingram, who had been talking to Weldon Granger, entered a demurrer. "What'll that prove?"

"The matter is still in my department," Cain said gently.

The district attorney opened his mouth, closed it, watched the collection of Mrs. Kampf's roomers file out in the wake of a reluctant Belarski. Cain dismissed the other dicks. Then with instructions to his secretary that he was not to be disturbed he led the way into his private office. That made only four of them that were left: Ingram, Granger, Rye and Cain himself. They arranged themselves in chairs. There was a stiff, belligerent silence.

After a while Cain said, looking directly at Rye, "There's something going on here that isn't quite kosher. We'd better straighten it out." With a charred forefinger he tamped tobacco into a pipe, lit it and leaned back comfortably. "Now then, we have two murders — we'll forget Ruiz for the moment — two murders which apparently are in some way connected. Have you any suggestions as to how they're connected?"

"Not if you leave out Ruiz," Rye said. "I think he did them."

"A convenient theory," Cain admitted drily. "Ruiz can't very well argue about it, can he?"

"No."

Cain looked fixedly at the ceiling. "I don't suppose it's possible you thought of that when you had him killed?"

"No." After a moment Rye said, angrily, "I didn't have him killed. I went into that room unarmed, because I knew damned well if anything happened and I had a gun — even padlocked in my pocket — it would be my gun that did it. So you see I took no chances."

Cain's eyes became slightly glacial. "I don't like that implication, Mr. Rye."

"Then don't make me say things like that."

Cain returned obliquely to the attack. "Do you think this girl had any connection with the man Ruiz?"

"I wouldn't know."

"Let's see, now, what was her name again?"

Rye's smile was that of a patient, long-suffering man. "I wouldn't know that, either." He looked intently at a sheaf of papers on Cain's desk. "Maybe if you ran through those, real carefully, you could find it." He thrust his chair violently backward and stood up. "Now if you're through playing mousy-mousy with me I'll stop bleeding all over your rug." He actually has his hand on the doorknob when Cain's telephone rang.

"Wait a minute," Cain said. He spoke into the phone and after a while said, "Oh, they're not? All right, thank you." He cradled the instrument with exact care. "The boys in the lab can't seem to find your fingerprints on that check."

Granger beat the air with his fists. "He used a handkerchief, I tell you! I remember now, he had a handkerchief in his hand when he — when he — " He sat down suddenly when the district attorney yanked his coat tails.

Cain pressed him a little. "Well, when he what?"

It was Floyd Ingram who answered that one. "It's perfectly obvious what happened, Inspector. The whole thing is a frame."

Rye took his hand off the doorknob. "You mean like Callahan's gun?"

"Now see here, Mr. Rye — "

"I won't see here," Rye said stubbornly. He looked at Cain. "Tell you what I will do, though. If Granger will sign a statement that he issued the check, and later saw Ruiz, not for the purpose of seeing justice done, but strictly as a political manoeuvre, I'll forget all about the check and where it was found." His mouth was unpleasant. "I don't care who you pin the murders on, just so it isn't Callahan."

Anger glinted in Cain's eyes. "I have nothing to do with what Mr. Granger does or does not sign. I'm conducting a murder investigation. And this office is conducted on the level, see?"

"Then go ahead and conduct it," Rye said nastily. "The elevator boy in Granger's office building will identify Ruiz as the man who threatened him with a pistol just before noon. I'll give you odds that the witness you were intending to trip me with will identify him as having been at Mrs. Kampf's rooming house. While there, at least the time I saw him, he also was waving a gun around. Later — tonight — he was discovered in the same room with Weldon Granger. Go ahead and laugh off the check if you want to. You've still got enough to build a better frame than you had against Callahan." He sneered at District Attorney Floyd Ingram. "At least you've got a motive. Granger wants to break Callahan as a means to breaking Quarrie."

Granger was sweating. "Are you suggesting that I hired this — this gunman to commit murder?"

"You suggested even worse than that," Rye said. "Why, Christ, you suggested that Callahan committed murder himself!" He gave Cain a level stare. "Fix it up any way you like, only tell Belarski to stop throwing his weight around. I'm getting sick of it." He went out.

In the emergency hospital downstairs he had his arm patched up. After that he telephoned for his car and while waiting for it snatched a bite at the Owl fountain diagonally across the corner. It was almost eight o'clock when he picked up Earl Holly, watching the Weldon Granger residence.

Holly's nerves were on edge. "I wish to Christ I'd never fingered her for you!"

"It wouldn't have made any difference," Rye said. "If you hadn't, somebody else would have. Or she would have, herself."

"What do you mean by that?"

"I don't know exactly," Rye said. Driving out to the Callahan house in Bel Air he brought Holly up to date on the Ruiz-Granger affair. There was a certain amount of satisfaction in his tone when he described the shooting. "It worked out pretty well, everything considered. I don't think Granger had time to get anything out of the Mex. If he had he'd have sprung it before this."

"The hell with that," Holly said angrily. "I want the girl."

"So do I," Rye said. He parked the car beneath the porte-cochere and got out. "We'll go find her presently."

"You mean you know where she is?"

"I think I know someone who does," Rye said. He went up the steps and rang the bell. Van Sweringen said that Callahan had been in but had gone out again. There had been no word from Gerald. Mrs. Callahan was upstairs, resting. "I'll talk to Mrs. Callahan," Rye said. Without relinquishing his hat he went up.

Sybil came to meet him, hands outstretched. She was in a rose satin negligee and there was color in her cheeks. "Oh, Bill, I've been so worried about you!"

He disengaged his hands. His dark eyes were bright and intent on her face. "Why?"

"Because — why, because Ed was worried about you, I suppose."

Rye shook his head. "You're not a very good liar, Sybil."

Doubt crept into her eyes, then something that could have been fear. "Don't look at me like that." She backed away from him a step, then another. "Bill, I didn't — "

"You did," Rye said. "You called the police and told them that there was a connection between the Small murder and the woman's. I want to know how you knew."

Sybil moistened parched lips, furtively. She forced herself to look at him. "What makes you think that I — that I would do a thing like that?"

"Because there's nobody else who knew that could have done it at the right time. The Small case was dying on its feet; Callahan was out and likely to stay out, unless something else happened to pop him back in again. I'll give you credit for trying, Sybil. You saw a chance to become a widow, a wealthy widow if the law did your work for you, and you helped things along." He put out a hand and caressed her white throat. "The only thing is, I told you to keep your mouth shut, remember?"

She began to tremble. "Bill, you can't know what you're saying!"

Deliberately he turned his back on her and went over to the front windows overlooking the street. "Happen to have a pair of field glasses, Sybil?"

"No. That is, I — "

"It doesn't matter," he said. "You could have gone out the side or the back and got his license number. I wouldn't put it past you, darling."

Her voice was choked. "Whose?"

"Small's," he said impatiently. "You asked me about the man I was talking to, remember?" Still not looking at her, he shook his head slightly, as though amazed at his own stupidity. "You've been watching for an opening for a long time and this looked like it might be it. You know I was lying when I said he was a plant to keep Ambrose off you." He sighed. "So you got his number, had it traced, located his office and tailed him to the rooming house out in Westlake." He turned and smiled at her. "You were smart, Sybil, only you weren't smart enough to know that I had everything else sewed up so that I'd know exactly where this last anonymous tip came from." He moved toward her leisurely, without haste. As though hypnotized, as though her feet were synchronized with his, she backed away from him until the chaise longue caught her behind the knees. She went down in a heap. He said casually, "I've some things to take care of, Sybil. I'll be back."

She uncovered her face. It was white and strained but no longer frightened. "Even if I'd killed them you couldn't prosecute me without pulling Callahan down." Fear returned to her as she saw the look in his eyes. "You couldn't — Bill!"

He nodded. "That's right, Sybil. I wasn't thinking about prosecuting you."

CHAPTER 19

THE apartment showed no signs of a struggle. Rye had hardly expected that it would. Patterson Powers was too clever to leave any loose ends laying around. He had said that Blossom Dee had run out with Gerald; therefore the apartment looked exactly as though she had decided to take a short trip, hastily but of her own free will. In the bedroom some rather nice clothes were tumbled carelessly about, and there were more empty hangers than there were clothes. In the luggage closet there were two unpacked bags. A thin film of dust was on them, and on the floor beside them, outlining the spot where a third had stood. Toilet articles were gone from the dressing room.

Holly's voice was petulant. "Well, what do we do now?" Holly had not subscribed to the theory that Powers might be using Blossom Dee's apartment as a hide-out for Carmelita. He did not believe that it was Powers who had taken her.

Rye was on his knees, sifting the contents of a wastebasket. He did not find anything that seemed pertinent to the case. Holly moved aimlessly but with growing irritation from one end of the apartment to the other. "I still don't see how you figure it was Powers."

Rye stood up, brushing at his knees a trifle absently. "He had her once. He's not the kind to accept the story I handed him this morning. He's more likely to have put a stake-out on the office, someone who saw me go in and Sherry come out." His eyes grew thoughtful. "No one followed us. Therefore someone must have followed Sherry. Powers knows Sherry."

"If you're so damned sure about it, why don't we quit stalling around and go take him apart?"

"Powers isn't the kind of guy you take apart," Rye said. "We could kill him. We couldn't make him talk." He lifted his head, listening. His eyes drew Holly's attention to the hall door. "I think we've got company."

They went into the living room, across that and into the tiny foyer. The doorknob was being tried, gently but inexpertly. Holly took up a position beside the door, back flat against the wall. Rye released the catch. Gerald Callahan, off balance, came in with the door and went to his knees at Rye's feet. There was a gun in his hand. Holly fell on him from the rear at the exact instant that Rye kicked him beneath the chin. Whatever Gerald had intended doing with the gun he forgot about. Rye bent and scooped it up and put it in his pocket. He was breathing a trifle gustily through his nose. "All right, let's haul him inside before some of the neighbors get curious." They carried him into the living room and deposited him on a davenport. Holly went back to lock the door. Rye stood looking down at the unconscious boy's face with neither affection nor dislike. Presently he took the gun out of his pocket and looked at that. It was the sort you can buy in almost any hockshop for five dollars. He was glad that Gerald had not walked in on someone else with it. The gun had no firing pin. He put it back in his pocket.

After a while the boy's eyelids fluttered open. Holly, at Rye's elbow, said disgustedly, "Now where the hell does *he* fit?"

"He's looking for Blossom too," Rye said.

Comprehension came into the boy's eyes. He sat erect, feeling of his jaw. "Where is she?"

"By me," Rye said. "I was hoping that maybe you would know.

You've been tagging around after Powers long enough to know more than I do about it."

Holly said nastily, "Don't let me annoy either of you, but which girl are we looking for? As far as I'm concerned Powers could have cut Miss Dee's throat and it would be all right with me."

Gerald pushed himself off the davenport and launched what was meant to be a devastating right fist at Holly's chin. Holly fended him off easily. "Be your age, punk." Gerald sat down and put his face in his hands.

Rye said, "You could follow some of your own advice, Earl. Looking for one is the same as looking for both. I don't think Powers has got more than a dozen spots he could use." He bent down and pulled Gerald's hands away from his face. "Listen, Gerry, I talked with Blossom the other night. I think she's on the level about you, but we can't work it out if you don't give us a little cooperation."

The boy's mouth was sullen. "What do you want to know?"

"Where you've been the last couple days; more particularly, where Pat Powers has been, and how the hell he's managed to miss you." He stared angry-eyed at nothing. "Tailing him as though you were going to a fire! It's a wonder you haven't been picked up in some gutter."

"I'm not afraid of him," Gerald muttered.

"No, you haven't got sense enough to be."

Slowly, haltingly, the youngest Callahan admitted that as a detective he hadn't been much good. "I was up here once before. The janitor let me in. I've tried all the places Blossom and I used to go together. I've watched Powers when I could, but there was some other girl he — "

Holly coughed. Until now he hadn't realized that Gerald didn't know who the other girl was. Rye kicked him in the shins. "So you saw the lights up here and came up?"

Gerald nodded. "I — I thought she might have come back."

Rye took the gun out of his pocket. "What were you going to do with this — shoot her?"

"No."

Rye looked at Holly. "All right, he doesn't know anything. We'll have to do the next best thing." He went to the phone and began calling numbers where he thought Powers might be located. Powers either owned or controlled half a dozen night spots. At each number he inquired not for Powers but for the gorilla named Joe. "Hello, is Joe around?"

"Joe who?"

"How many Joes has Pat got working for him?"

After the third or fourth try he found out that Joe's last name was Riordan. He did not find anybody who had seen Joe since about one o'clock that afternoon. Pretending that he was Joe he now began inquiring for Powers, presently discovering that Powers was in his office above the Club Paradise. Nobody called him a liar for being Joe, not even the man he talked to at the Paradise. He hung up and looked at Holly and Gerald. He rather wished he could tie Gerald up somewhere, but on the whole that didn't look so good. The hoax he hoped to perpetrate might go sour; Powers might decide to come up here instead. He said, "There's a chance you can turn out to be a hero even yet, Gerry. You'll have to keep your head."

The boy stood up. "I'm ready." His face was pale, his eyes bloodshot, but at least he wasn't drunk.

"We'll have to pick up a gun for you," Rye said. "One that really shoots." He looked at Holly. "He'll ride with you. If this works, you and he can tail Powers from in front. I'll tag along behind. That way, if one of us loses him the other will be on the plant."

Holly was skeptical. "What are you going to do?"

"When we're set," Rye said, "I'm going to be a guy named Joe and talk to Powers himself. It'll sound — I hope — like something terrible has happened to me."

* * * * *

It was almost inconceivable that so secluded a retreat could be found within a hundred yards of one of the city's main boulevards. Perhaps the time of year had something to do with it, or the name of the rustic lane itself. It was called Road's End. Giant peppers and oaks bordered the lane on either side and climbed steeply ascending slopes to ridges tall and ragged against a starlit sky. Down here on the floor of the canyon it was darker than Ethiopia in a blackout. In a small clearing fenced by a stake-and-rider effect of hand-split logs sat a house, also of logs, a patently artificial hunting lodge from which nobody had ever hunted. The windows were boarded up, but not tightly enough so that it couldn't be seen that there were lights within. A faint wind stirred the trees and dispersed the barely perceptible smoke issuing from one of the two cobblestone chimneys. Somewhere near at hand water rippled over rocks. There was no other sound.

From the shelter of a tree twice his own thickness Rye watched the house and waited for Patterson Powers to come back. Powers had not stopped at the house. He and his car were somewhere up ahead, deeper in the canyon. Powers was playing it close to his vest. He had been in a hurry, but not so great a hurry that he was unmindful of the possibility of a trap. Rye saw with the pleased satisfaction of one who has guessed right that there were no telephone wires leading into the building. Powers had been unable to call back and find out exactly what had happened to Joe.

Sharply in the stillness a twig snapped. The sound came from the direction of the mouth of the canyon. Rye cursed Holly and Gerald impartially. Tailing Powers' car from in front they had gone on past the lane. Rye too had passed it, turning a quarter mile beyond and coming back to leave his car in a ditch at the side of the highway. Presumably they had done the same. The snapping twig was the first sign he had had of their immediate presence. Then he saw that it was neither Holly nor Gerald who had stepped on it. Powers had circled the house, probably high up among the trees, and was coming along the lower reach of the lane on foot. Rye knew that it was Powers only by the bulk of the shadow. The man was stalking the house as carefully as Rye himself.

Powers' shadow merged with that of the split-rail fence, and rusty hinges protested as the gate was opened. Powers retreated to a tree almost as large as Rye's, waiting. The front door of the house suddenly yawned wide, spewing yellow light out over the porch. In the opening Joe Riordan stood shading his eyes, trying to penetrate the surrounding darkness. "I thought I heard somep'n."

Rye fell on Powers from behind. There was a brief, vicious struggle for possession of Powers' gun. A couple of shots racketed back and forth in the canyon. The front door slammed. Presently Rye stood up, saying jerkily, "Be nice, Pat. We don't want any more to happen than already has happened."

Gerald came running up, waving his gun. "I don't think we hit anybody."

"Where's Holly?"

"Covering the back door." Gerald discovered Patterson Powers on his knees at the base of the tree. "You lousy bastard!"

In the darkness Powers' voice had the sound of dry husks. "All right, Rye, you win. What do you want?"

"The girls are in there?"

"Yes."

Rye held the gun negligently at his side. "Then tell Joe the fireworks are all over."

CHAPTER 20

IN the kitchenette of Rye's apartment Sherry McKay was making coffee. In the living room, Carmelita, small and pale and shy, sat with her legs curled up under her at an extreme end of the chesterfield and watched Callahan, sitting stiff and straight and uncomfortable at the other. Earl Holly, obviously wanting to sit between them but restrained by one of his few nobler impulses, wandered rather aimlessly around, picking things up, putting them down again. Rye straddled a straight chair and leaned folded arms on its back, chin resting on his arms, dark eyes bright and intent on the girl's face. "Powers get anything out of you?"

She shook her head. "No."

"I didn't think he would," Rye said.

Callahan looked at the palm of one large, powerful hand. "You made a mistake letting him go."

"I made a friend," Rye said. After a while he said, "In politics you need all the friends you can get. Hanging a kidnap rap on him wouldn't have done anybody any good."

Callahan gnawed at his mustache. "Where's Gerald?"

"Off somewhere with Blossom."

"And Powers is going to stand for that?"

"That was part of the bargain," Rye said.

"Well by God, I'm not going to stand for it," Callahan said angrily. "She's nothing but a tramp."

"All right," Rye said, "then Gerald is going to marry a tramp. You might as well make up your mind to it."

Sherry came in with a tray. "What are you two fighting about now?" She was in green tonight, and that made her eyes green too. Her dark hair held only the faintest tinge of mahogany. She and Rye appeared to be the only self-possessed people in the room. "Callahan thinks Blossom Dee is a tramp," Rye said. "He's led such a sweet life himself that he's eligible to criticise." He looked at Carmelita. "Do you think she's a tramp, querida mia?"

She blushed prettily. "To the man Joe and the others she used the language of a tramp. To me she did not." She shot a fleeting glance at Callahan's profile. "To me she was kind. I do not think she is a tramp."

Rye accepted a cup of coffee and sipped at it. "You see?" He smiled at the restlessly pacing Holly. "Sit down, Earl." He began to talk in a carefully emotionless voice about El Segundo Ruiz. "There was a man for you — thorough, painstaking, callous enough to do what had to be done, cautious enough to wait when waiting seemed necessary."

"But you caught him," Callahan said.

"Yes, I caught him," Rye admitted. "Largely because an element had been introduced that he did not foresee; that he could not have foreseen." He sighed a little. "Powers."

The telephone rang. He went to it, said, "Yes. . . . All right. . . . Yes," hung up and returned to his chair. "That was our worthy opponent, Mr. Weldon Granger. He will sign a little paper I asked him to if I forget about a check of his that was found on Ruiz." He was vaguely uncomfortable under Sherry's eyes. "No, Powers' grudge against Gerald, his desire to get some kind of a hold on me to force me to produce Gerald, was something that Ruiz could not have anticipated. Without Carmelita, without hearing from her, Ruiz was lost. His only hope was a quick clean-up from Granger."

There was a sort of palpitant silence. Earl Holly said in a low tight voice, "Just how did you mean that — without hearing from her? Do you mean that he was *expecting* to hear from her?"

"Of course," Rye said. He appeared surprised. "Hadn't you guessed that they were working together?" He waited till Holly's gun was half out of its holster before he got up rather swiftly and took it away from him. His left arm pinned the younger man to him. "Be nice, Earl." After a while he stepped away and looked at the others. Carmelita was motionless, exactly as she had been. Her eyes were a little wider, that was all. Callahan's square face had the grayish pallor of a very old man's. His hands were knotted into fists. Sherry's coffee cup rattled against the saucer. "Bill, you can't do this to her. Not even to save him!"

Rye sat on the padded arm of a club chair, dangling the gun by its trigger guard between his knees. "Would you write something for me, Carmelita?"

She moistened her lips. "What?"

"Anything," Rye said. "Anything at all." He lifted his eyes to Sherry's. "Get a pen and some paper, hon."

Sherry didn't move. Rye looked at Holly. "Earl?"

"No."

"All right, then I'll do it," Rye said. Careful not to turn his back on any of them he went over to the wall console and got paper and pen out of the drawer. He left the drawer a little way open. "Write something, Carmelita."

Her voice was a puzzled child's. "Why should I?"

"Because I think it was you who wrote the letter, chiquita." The tiny muscle at the corner of Rye's mouth began to twitch. "You have two choices. If you don't write I'll know you're afraid to. If you do, what you write can be compared with the letter."

She struck his hand aside. "I hate you!" She appealed to the others. "Earl, you 'ave said you love me. Mr. Callahan — father — " Her voice broke and she wept, not noisily. "Do not let him do this thing to me!"

Callahan's cry was a tortured thing. "I'll see him in hell first!" He stood up, putting his bulk between Rye and the girl. "You don't need that, Bill. We can — I tell you I won't stand for it."

Holly's face was white and drawn. "You'd better talk fast, Bill.

Gun or no gun, if you try anything like that I'm going to take you apart."

Sherry McKay said nothing at all.

"I know," Rye said. "You think this is a frame. You think because I framed other things — " His voice hardened. "If Carmelita isn't afraid, let her write."

She thrust Callahan aside and stood there proud and straight before him. "Carmelita is afraid of nothing!"

"You're good," Rye said. "You're very good. I told you that once before, only about something else." After a moment, not addressing anyone in particular, he bagan to talk in a low, monotonous voice. "This was a blackmail scheme with a new twist. They had nothing to start with except the knowledge that Callahan had been in Mexico and that he had known a woman named Carmel Machado. Ruiz was married to her. Carmelita — Well, God knows who her father really was. It was not Callahan." His face was suddenly etched with deep lines. "Callahan was chosen to be her father simply because he had money and was a public figure."

Carmelita spat at him. "Liar!" She crept into the shelter of Callahan's arm. "He is lying, Señor — father. You and I, we feel it that we are one, no?"

Rye went on as though there had been no interruption. "So they had nothing they could really back up with proof. They didn't need it at first. They figured the probabilities and Callahan's own conscience would start the ball rolling." For the first time in moments he looked directly at the girl. "The forwarding addresses on the envelope of the letter — they can be checked, you know. They will show that at each place the man Ruiz stayed, probably under the name of Edward Callahan. The letter was mailed again and again, to give it authenticity, until the time was ripe to spring it on the right Callahan." His eyes were muddy. "That would be about the time that Lou Small stole Callahan's gun for you."

Holly cursed him. "So now Small was in it too!"

"And Mrs. Kampf," Rye said. Lean brown fingers twirled the cylinder on the gun between his knees. "I don't know just when it occurred to me that it was funny Ruiz could have located the girl so easily." He thought about that. "Probably when I noticed for the first time what a peculiar lot of roomers the old lady had. They just weren't the type to go with her front of tatting collars and Gideon Bibles."

Callahan growled deep down in his throat. "Just who are you trying to protect with this preposterous story?" His arm tightened protectively around the girl.

"You," Rye said. "Myself." His lips drew back over his teeth in a grimace of distaste. "There comes a time when you have to hand the police something besides stories and perjured witnesses. This is the time. Belarski and Cain and Ingram are on their way up. I'm handing them the girl."

"Over my dead body!" Holly shouted. He hurled himself at the gun in Rye's hands. Rye stood up and with his left fist hit Holly high up on the temple. The coffee table, cups and saucers crashed under Holly's weight. He lay there a moment, unmoving. Sherry McKay put a hand to her throat, watching Rye with eyes that were filled with horror, Carmelita clung to Calalhan, a frightened child.

Rye said woodenly, "All of you might as well make up your minds to listen to me. I've been as big a sucker as anybody and it isn't doing my ego any good to admit it." From the corner of his eye he watched Sherry's face, finding little comfort there. "As I told you, Ruiz and the girl didn't have anything to start with. I searched her effects and those of the man. There weren't even the scraps of letters they talked about." He drew an uneven breath. "Here's what happened; here's exactly what happened, because it's the only way the whole thing fits: Ruiz, the girl, Lou Small and Old Lady Kampf' were all in it together. The letter was the come-on. From that we were led to accepting Lou Small, who probably stole the gun from Callahan's library the very night I first ran into him. He didn't know the kind of people he was playing with. He thought he was smart enough to handle them."

Carmelita stood free of Callahan's arm, as though no longer needing its support. Rye admired her. "You're good, chiquita. You're one of the finest actresses it's ever been my misfortune to meet." He looked at his watch. It was ten o'clock. "The visits to the other detective agencies were arranged, Lou Small himself pointing out those he had connections with and who would recommend him."

His eyes held no affection when he put them on Callahan. "The gag was new insofar as Carmelita was never to ask you for a dime. She wanted nothing but revenge, and it was only gradually that she allowed herself to be talked out of that. It was Ruiz, the cruel, unscrupulous step-father, we all had to fear; the man she herself appeared to be running away from." Again and elaborately he admired the girl. "Every step, every move was carefully planned. Even throwing the pistol away that you knew I had seen. I was supposed to have softened you up to the point where you could no longer go through with your original scheme for revenge. Running away from me, and later from Powers, made the perfect picture of the frightened, confused little girl. It also gave you the opportunity to contact Ruiz and let him know how things were progressing."

Holly's voice was choked. "You mean she actually let me tail her to that hotel?"

"You didn't have any difficulty, did you?" Rye's eyes grew bright and hard. "That was the pay-off — the sobbing girl in a shabby, fifth-rate hotel room, a girl who didn't know which way to turn except to the man she'd convinced was her father." Rye spat. "And even he was a murderer!" His eyes got that oddly muddy look again. "It had even me on the ropes."

"Then she knew I was out in the hall all the time?"

Rye nodded. "Just as she knew I'd be around when Pat Powers hired her away from Izzy Arnstein. That was some more of the same. She hated me; she believed her father had murdered Lou Small; she never wanted to see either of us again." He went over and put a hand under her chin. "Was it you who shot Small — or Ruiz?"

She didn't even tremble at his touch. "You know it was not I, Señor. Why do you do this so horrible a thing to me?"

Rye shook his head. "No, darling, I don't. You probably did it when you ran away from Holly the first time — the time you ditched the pistol." He withdrew his hand. "It was the gun that confused me — Callahan's gun. At that time I believed in you. Callahan's identification made be believe in you further." He smiled at her. "Do you suppose, little one, that if I didn't know what I was talking about; if all these things weren't capable of proof; I'd let the cops have you?"

She shivered then, and backed away from him. "I hate you!"

"Of course. Callahan hates me, Holly hates me, everybody hates me." He sighed a little. "And none of them has as much reason as you. It's your neck I'm putting the rope around."

"You won't. You wouldn't dare!"

"I will and I would, chiquita." Deliberately he turned his back on her. "You haven't a thing except that Callahan once knew your mother — if she was your mother." And then, very swiftly, he turned again and knocked the gun out of her hand; the gun she had gotten from the open drawer of the console. He encircled her in a strong arm, holding her tightly to him, and looked over her head at Holly. "Satisfied, Earl? You, Ed?" He did not look at Sherry.

Holly's eyes were sick. Callahan sank heavily to the chesterfield and put his face in his hands. "Bill, I—It just doesn't seem possible!"

There was an authoritative knock on the door. As it opened and Belarski and Cain and Floyd Ingram came in Carmelita broke from Rye's grip and ran for the windows. Rye lifted his gun but apparently the mechanism was jammed. He did not fire. Belarski taken off guard, fumbled his first shot and by that time it was all over. Sash and screen went out under the impact of Carmelita's body, then she was gone. An eerie, high-pitched scream lasted for perhaps three seconds. Then that too was gone.

It was Inspector Cain who presently turned from the shattered window. "Seven stories," he said in his dry, precise voice. He went to the telephone, picked it up, turned to look at Belarski's livid face. "You'd better go down and keep the crowd back, Lieutenant."

"It's a frame!" Belarski shouted. "He deliberately let her get away. He's as guilty as anybody else in this thing."

Rye looked at him. "I haven't forgotten what you and your boy friends did to me last night, Nick. This is as good a time as any for me to even that up."

Cain said sharply, "Belarski, do as you're told!"

Belarski went out. Cain said, "And you, Rye, I don't mind telling you that I'm half of that opinion myself." Frowning, he gave the number of Headquarters. His face was that of a middle-aged, quietly annoyed bookkeeper's.

Floyd Ingram pompously cleared his throat as a prelude to, "Now see here, Mr. Rye, there is a great deal about this case with which I am not satisfied." His tone grew even more irritable. "Not satisfied at all."

"In fact there's a great deal you don't even understand," Rye said.

"Then perhaps you'd better tell me, sir!"

"All right." Rye waited till Cain had finished with the phone. "The girl killed Small. She as good as admitted it. I had just finished taking a gun away from her when you came in." The toe of his right shoe prodded the gun gently where it lay on the rose-beige carpet. "You ought to find her fingerprints on it."

"And Ruiz killed this — ah — Mrs. Kampf?"

"Yes."

"Why?"

Rye made an impatient gesture. "They'd both served their purpose. When they were no longer needed they'd have been just a couple of extra mouths to feed."

Ingram was persistent. "But the Kampf murder wasn't to be saddled on Mr. Callahan here?"

"Neither was the Small kill," Rye said. "Not really. They meant to scare Callahan, yes, but he wouldn't have done them any good dead. I think they rather counted on me to get him off. If I hadn't, I've no doubt the girl would have fingered Ruiz for the job. That would have left only her to enjoy the gravy."

"Then she was really the brains of the gang?"

Rye looked the district attorney straight in the eye. "Isn't that as good a theory as any? You wouldn't want Granger to be it, would you?"

Ingram's mouth opened and closed a couple of times without any sound coming out. It was Cain who put the question Rye had been waiting for. "What was it they had on Callahan?"

"The murder of Lou Small."

A faint flush came into Cain's face. His eyes were angry. "And before that? The thing that induced Callahan to go to Small's office?"

Rye smiled. "Now you're trying to stick me for bribery." He shook his head from side to side. "Callahan went there several weeks ago — to see a chiropractor about a twisted ankle."

Something that could have been admiration replaced the anger in Cain's eyes. "But off the record?"

Rye looked at the district attorney. "Off the record?"

"Yes."

Rye bent and picked up a coffee cup that had not been broken in Holly's crash. "You couldn't prove anything anyway. That Knebel guy is as hard as nails." After a while he said, "All right, then, it's a rather delicate matter and I wouldn't want it to go any farther. A guy named Walter Ambrose had gotten some pictures and was trying to sell them to Callahan through Small."

One of Cain's rare profanities escaped him. "So you were responsible for that too!"

Rye's eyes were clear and bright and slightly amused. "For what?"

"Skip it," Cain said wearily. He stared at Ingram. "Well, as long as it doesn't have to go to court I guess we've got enough, eh?"

The district attorney admitted sadly that they had enough. "I don't suppose there would be any use probing into the past of these — ah — people?"

"It's all right with me," Rye said. "I'd suggest that you didn't probe too hard. Granger might not like it."

"See here, young man, are you suggesting — "

"I just said he *might* not like it."

Earl Holly began looking around for his hat. "I think I'll go out and get stinking drunk. It's one hell of a lousy world."

A disillusioned and slightly sick Callahan got up off the chesterfield. "I think I'll join you, son." They went out with Inspector Cain and the district attorney.

After a long, long time Sherry got down on her knees and began picking up the pieces of the shattered coffee service. "I suppose you're very proud of yourself?"

Rye's mouth was bitter. "Proud!" He deliberately scratched a match across the polished surface of the mahogany console. "Because Powers copped the girl from under our noses? Because Ruiz, not hearing from her, thought she might have crossed him up too and went to Granger?" He lit a cigarette and snapped the match at the yawning window through which the girl had flung herself. "What the hell have I got to be proud of?"

She looked up at him and he saw that her eyes were wet. She brushed angrily at them with the back of her hand. "Then nothing is changed? Everything is just the same as it was?"

He nodded gloomily. "The Callahan tribe will always be the same. Gerald, for the moment, has got what he thinks he wants. For all I know, she may be good for him. Sybil is — well, Sybil is scared enough to be good for a while." He sighed. "As for Callahan, he'll always be what he is and there's nothing I can do about it." He too got down on his knees and began picking up the pieces. It occurred to him that there was something almost symbolic about that. "You wouldn't want me to talk myself out of a job, would you?"

She turned on him rather fiercely. "I'd love it!"

He had to stoop a little to kiss her on the cheek. His eyes were sombre. "Don't nag me, Sherry."

"Nag you!" She turned furious eyes on him. "Do you think I enjoy every cop in town beating up on you? Is this supposed to be fun for me?" Her chin quivered a little but she still refused to come into his arms. "Killing and lying and cheating and all for what? For politics? For an Irish immigrant that couldn't write his own name until he was twenty? For a man who isn't fit to shine your shoes?"

"Oh, Christ," Rye said tiredly, "I might as well be in love with Belarski." He rocked back on his heels. "You know something, hon? I've been thinking about an island somewhere down in the South Seas. It wouldn't have to be much of an island. Just you and me and a little island."

"You know darned well you wouldn't go there!"

He turned and pillowed his head in her lap. His eyes for the first time in days were at peace. "Well, no," he admitted, "but there's no harm in thinking about it, is there?"

THE END